'I asked the

Lauren stared ... moment. 'You a...

'You've got it in one, honey,' he drawled lazily.

'I don't understand. Why would you do that?'

'I don't know. Maybe it was because you did such a good job interviewing me the last time—remember?'

'You mean that you wanted someone to report your marriage without sensationalising it and you thought I was a fairly safe bet.'

Dear Reader

A new year is starting and now is the time to think about the kind of stories you've enjoyed reading during the past year and the stories you would like to read throughout this coming year. As Valentine's Day approaches, why not dream up the most perfect romantic evening for yourself? No doubt it will include a sprinkling of charm, a good degree of atmosphere, a healthy amount of passion and love, and of course your favourite Mills & Boon novel. Keep romance close to your heart—make this year special!

The Editor

Kathryn Ross was born in Zambia where her parents happened to live at that time. Educated in Ireland and England, she now lives in a village near Blackpool, Lancashire. Kathryn is a professional beauty therapist, but writing is her first love. As a child she wrote adventure stories and at thirteen was editor of her school magazine. Happily, ten writing years later 'Designed with Love' was accepted by Mills & Boon. A romantic Sagittarian, she loves travelling to exotic locations.

Recent titles by the same author:

PLAYING BY THE RULES

BY LOVE ALONE

BY

KATHRYN ROSS

MILLS & BOON LIMITED
ETON HOUSE   18-24 PARADISE ROAD
RICHMOND   SURREY   TW9 1SR

All the characters in this book have no existence outside the imagination of the Author, and have no relation whatsoever to anyone bearing the same name or names. They are not even distantly inspired by any individual known or unknown to the Author, and all the incidents are pure invention.

All Rights Reserved. The text of this publication or any part thereof may not be reproduced or transmitted in any form or by any means, electronic or mechanical, including photocopying, recording, storage in an information retrieval system, or otherwise, without the written permission of the publisher.

This book is sold subject to the condition that it shall not, by way of trade or otherwise, be lent, resold, hired out or otherwise circulated without the prior consent of the publisher in any form of binding or cover other than that in which it is published and without a similar condition including this condition being imposed on the subsequent purchaser.

*First published in Great Britain 1992
by Mills & Boon Limited*

© Kathryn Ross 1992

*Australian copyright 1992
Philippine copyright 1993
This edition 1993*

ISBN 0 263 77900 9

*Set in Times Roman 10 on 11¼ pt.
01-9302-56389 C*

Made and printed in Great Britain

CHAPTER ONE

'I DON'T want to cover the story.' Lauren's gentle voice was like a bombshell in the silence of the office.

Warren Peters stared at her as if she were some alien that had descended on his newspaper from outer space. 'What the hell are you saying?' he asked after a moment's nasty silence.

'Warren, you know I can't do this, and you know why.' She tried very hard to remain calm, but it was hard. Panic was welling up inside her.

'No, I don't, Lauren—perhaps you would like to explain it to me.' Her editor's voice had an ominous ring to it now. 'We have been offered an exclusive interview, a scoop, with a man who is a legend in his own time, a man whom the media are falling over themselves to get near, and you don't want to cover it. I'd be very interested to hear your reasons.'

'You know my reasons. You know I was... involved with Cole Adams.' At one time it had seemed as if the whole world knew about her and Cole. Her name had been spread across every one of the tabloids. She pushed back a strand of blonde hair with a hand that was not entirely steady, and stared at the elderly man who sat on the opposite side of the large desk, her blue eyes wide and unconsciously pleading.

Warren Peters felt a momentary pang of sympathy for her which he immediately squashed. If he got this story he was looking at a major circulation-boost for the paper, one that would make its proprietor very, very happy. 'That was yesterday's news,' he stated in a dry tone.

For a moment pain was clearly visible in the eloquent blue eyes before she lowered dark lashes. 'Yes.' Her voice was barely audible. Warren was a tough city editor; she should have known better than to make an appeal so blatantly based on pure emotion.

'We're living in a goldfish bowl, Lauren; if everyone refused to tackle a story because they knew someone who was involved, news would dwindle dramatically. We have a professional duty to set aside personal feelings and report to the public. That is what being a journalist is all about.'

'I don't need a lecture on how to do my job, Warren,' she murmured, a hint of annoyance in her tone now. But she was annoyed with herself, not her editor, because deep down she knew he was right. She was behaving like a scared emotional female, not a professional journalist. Just what was so frightening about seeing Cole again? she asked herself rationally and tried to ignore the shiver of apprehension that raced down her spine.

'Where is he?' she asked cautiously. 'At his London home? Or is he in California?'

'Neither. He's shooting the video for his latest album, *An Ancient Law*, out in Thailand.'

'I see.' Lauren frowned. 'So you want me to fly out and interview him while he's there?'

Warren smiled. 'Not a bad assignment, is it? You'll be missing some of London's cold grey January weather and jetting off to the sun,' he drawled persuasively.

A ghost of a smile lit her delicate features for a moment. 'That sounds like a bribe, Warren. What's the angle? Am I just doing a straightforward piece on Cole Adams, sex symbol and pop star, or have you something else in mind?'

'Am I to take it you've come to your senses and are willing to take the assignment?' her boss countered drily.

'Have I a choice?' Her blue eyes met his steadily and directly.

'There is always a choice.'

Lauren didn't think she liked the implications in that gravel-deep tone. Was he giving her an ultimatum—do your job or get out and don't waste my time? She bit down on the softness of her lower lip. Damn Cole Adams. He had nearly wrecked her life once before; she wouldn't allow him to do it again. 'When do you want me to leave?' she asked firmly before she could change her mind.

'Soon as possible,' Warren said quickly, a look of triumph on his lined face. 'You'll have to get the necessary injections plus a visa.'

Lauren nodded. 'Who am I taking with me?'

'No one. Adams has stipulated that he doesn't want a photographer. I didn't push the issue. He was very firm and I had a feeling we would lose the story if I pressed him.'

Lauren frowned. 'We need pictures. The story will sell twice as well with them.' She was silent for a while as she thought things through. Photographs of Cole would sell more newspapers, but there was another reason she wanted to take a photographer. She didn't want to be alone when she saw Cole again. 'I'll take Jon,' she said firmly after a moment.

'I don't know, Lauren...he won't be pleased,' Warren said hesitantly.

Lauren shrugged. She didn't care a damn whether Cole was pleased or not. 'I presume you *are* sending me on this assignment because I know Cole,' she stated drily. 'So just leave me to sort out the question of photographs with him. I'm sure we can come to some arrangement.' It was amazing how confident she sounded, when inside her stomach was churning with apprehension.

Warren nodded and looked very pleased now.

'OK, now that's sorted out, what's the story-line—Cole Adams, millionaire super-star? Or Cole Adams, the man women love to love?' There was just a hint of bitterness in her carefully modulated voice.

Warren didn't seem to have heard her for a moment; he was busy rifling through the papers on his desk. 'What?' He glanced up. 'Oh, didn't I tell you? Adams is getting married out there as soon as he's finished work on the video. We're getting the exclusive story.'

'Getting married,' Lauren murmured dazedly, and for a moment her stomach felt as if it were in free fall. 'I don't believe it.'

Warren glanced at her from beneath bushy grey eyebrows. 'That information is strictly hush-hush, but I assure you it's correct. I have it direct from Adams himself. He wouldn't tell me who the woman in question is, or where or when the ceremony is to take place. Just that we should have a reporter out at the Bangkok Sheldon no later than end of the month.' Warren started to delve into the papers in front of him again. 'Ah, here we are.' He passed a folder across to her. 'I've looked back at some of the recent stories we've run on Adams and come up with two possibilities as to who his intended bride could be. I've put a photo of both in there, plus a brief résumé. Have a look and see what you think.'

Lauren wasn't capable of any rational thought but somehow she did manage to take the file and get stiffly to her feet. Pride was the only thing that kept her features firmly set in an unemotional mask.

It wasn't until later, when she opened the file in private, that the mask slipped and she tore the glossy photo of the beautiful brunette into a hundred tiny pieces. That was what she thought of Cole's marriage to Donna Wade.

* * *

Lauren stepped out of the shower and reached for a white towel, to wrap it firmly around her slender figure. The forceful jet of water had refreshed her and she no longer felt like crawling into bed and sleeping around the clock. She took another towel and briskly rubbed her long hair. Then she studied her reflection in the bathroom mirror. She didn't care for what she saw.

Her skin was far too pale and her blue eyes seemed to dominate her small face. She was twenty-six and a successful career woman, yet she looked like a little girl, a waif dragged in from the storm. The idea made her lips curve, and the humour that at one time had never been far from her blue eyes returned for a moment to make them sparkle. 'Fool,' she berated herself silently and, taking her silk wrap from the back of the door, she stepped out into the luxury of her hotel bedroom.

She took a bottle of mineral water from the fridge and poured some out, then crossed to the doors leading out to the balcony, flicking the radio on on the way past.

After the air-conditioned cool of her room, it was a surprise to step out into a blast of warm air. Even though the sun had gone down over an hour ago, the heat of the night was intense. She glanced down at the terrace below her. White tables laid with white damask cloths, gleaming silver cutlery and flickering candle-light overlooked the dark gleaming water of the Chao Phraya River that snaked its way through the heart of Bangkok.

She sipped the cool mineral water and stared down at the empty terrace. London seemed another world away, the long flight that she had just taken seemed like a distant dream, everything felt slightly unreal. The heady scent of bougainvillaea invaded the heat of the night, from the room behind she could hear the radio playing a dreamy ballad. For a moment she felt more relaxed than she had in weeks.

The music slowed a little and the heavy beat of the music changed subtly. The deep, husky voice that invaded the night now was like velvet to the ears. It conjured up the image of an incredibly sexy man, the type that a woman dreamed of. Lauren stood perfectly still, wrapped in the warm cocoon of memories that song and that voice conjured up. Cole Adams had a voice that sent shivers of delight racing down a woman's spine. Lauren swallowed hard and remembered how he had sung that song just for her, how they had laughed together in the Californian sunshine when the record had been a number one hit. 'That song is just for you, Laurie, my love, my life.' For a moment she could hear those whispered words again so plainly that it was almost as if Cole was standing next to her. A shaft of pain hit her heart, so painful, so intense that she gasped aloud. The glass she was holding fell from nerveless fingers and smashed on the cool tiles beneath her feet.

For a breathless second all she could think of was getting to the radio and switching it off. Even when his voice was gone and there was only silence in the room, her heartbeat refused to go back to normal. Her hands were shaking, her mouth felt dry. She took deep shuddering breaths and willed herself to get back into control. If just hearing his voice did that to her, how was she going to meet with him tomorrow and interview him in the cool, businesslike way she had been rehearsing all week? Panic filled her and she hated herself for it. Why should the thought of seeing Cole affect her so deeply? As Warren had so rightly said, they were yesterday's news; she shouldn't feel like this.

A tap on her door brought her thoughts sharply back to the present. That would be Jon; she had promised to have dinner with him down on the terrace. She glanced at her watch and grimaced. She hadn't realised that it was so late. Galvanised into action, she picked up the blue silk dress she had laid out earlier and made towards the bathroom. 'Come on in, Jon,' she called over her shoulder. 'I won't be long.'

She heard the door open and close as she pulled the dress over her head. She glanced at her reflection. The blue silk looked cool and very feminine. Her blonde hair had dried naturally into long silky curls. She applied a soft colour to her lips and pulled her fingers through her hair before stepping back into the bedroom. 'Sorry about that—I——' She came to an abrupt halt in the doorway, her eyes locking on the powerfully handsome man who stood next to her bed. 'Cole!' Her voice was a mere whisper in the silence of the room.

Eyes as dark as his name swept over her slender body. For a moment she wondered if she was hallucinating. She closed her eyes and opened them again, but he was still there. Still the most attractive man she had ever met. There was something about Cole's rugged looks that was disturbingly sensual. Her heart pounded painfully against her chest as her eyes moved hungrily over that familiar broad-shouldered frame, dressed in a casually smart lightweight suit. For one mad second she longed to go into those arms; she could remember so clearly how good it had felt to be held by him.

'Hello, Laurie.' The deep, husky voice made her hands clench with the effort of keeping all her emotions tightly in check. 'It's nice to see you again.'

Nice... her brain seized the words and danced them angrily around inside the corridors of pain inside her.

'I wish I could say the same,' she answered tightly.

For a moment an expression flickered across those strong features that she couldn't decipher. Then it was gone and he merely shrugged. 'So, you're still angry with me. I thought by now——'

'Cole what are you doing in here?' She cut across him quickly before the conversation could get to a personal level.

One dark eyebrow lifted. 'As you've just flown a few thousand miles to see me, I thought the least I could do was take the elevator down a few floors to welcome you.'

'You make it sound as if I wanted to come,' she murmured in a tone that was icy. 'I'm not making a social visit, Cole. I'm here because the *Global Record* sent me, no other reason.'

The dark rugged face was impassive. 'I know; I was the one who asked them to send you.'

She stared at him with perplexity for a moment. 'You asked specifically for me?'

'You've got it in one, honey,' he drawled lazily.

She shook her head. She had wondered why Cole had chosen to give his story to the *Record* when he knew she worked there, but she had never in a million years thought she was the reason. 'I don't understand. Why would you do that?'

There was silence for a moment. His eyes moved over the delicate lines of her face, lingered on the soft curve of her lips. He hesitated, then shrugged. 'Hell, I don't know. Maybe it was because you did such a good job interviewing me the last time—remember?'

She could feel heat surging up under her skin. That was something that she didn't want to remember. She didn't make any reply; she couldn't find any flippant words. She couldn't make light of a time that had once meant so much to her.

'You're good at your job, Lauren,' he said gently. 'I know anything you write about me will be fair comment. Maybe that's why I asked for you, hmm?'

'You mean that you wanted someone to report your marriage without sensationalising it out of all proportion and you thought I was a fairly safe bet.' There was no hint of emotion in her perfectly modulated voice, but inside there was a seething mass of feeling that was fighting for release. Maybe she could understand his reason for wanting her to report his marriage. Their relationship was over, they had both agreed that six months ago. So why couldn't she be as practical as Cole about this? He was giving her an exclusive story; she in turn should do her best to see it was treated in a professional manner.

'Lauren, I...' He trailed off and raked an impatient hand through his thick, dark hair. 'Hell, this is harder than I thought it would be.'

Her lips curved into a smile that was at best tremulous. 'Don't worry, Cole. You were right to give me the story and I will handle it...professionally.' She swallowed hard and forced herself to look up at him with cool clear eyes. 'By the way, I should offer you my congratulations. I suppose the lucky lady is——'

'We'll save the talk about my forthcoming marriage until you are interviewing me, shall we?' he cut across her suddenly, his voice gravel-deep.

She frowned. 'Well, maybe I'm interviewing you now, Cole; you know a good journalist never switches off, and now seems as good a time as any to ask——'

'Take it from me, Lauren, now is not a good time.' His voice had steely undertones. 'I came down here to ask you to come have dinner with me. My forthcoming marriage is not on the agenda for conversation. I think we should sit down as friends and just talk.'

'I don't think that's a good idea, Cole.' Despite all her efforts, her voice was not very steady now.

'Why not?' The dark eyes seemed to be boring right into her very soul.

'Because... because I don't think we have anything to say to each other.' She looked away from the dark, intense eyes, her heart thumping painfully. 'Besides, I don't think your wife-to-be would be very keen on the idea of us dining together.'

'Well, you've got something right,' he agreed drily. 'She doesn't seem very keen at all.'

That didn't surprise Lauren. Donna had never made any secret of the fact that she didn't like her. But then she could hardly blame the woman. She had been in love with Cole long before Lauren had arrived on the scene. 'So it's probably best for all concerned if we keep this strictly business. There's no point in us pretending to be just good friends when we both know perfectly well that's something we could never be.'

One dark eyebrow lifted. 'Why not, Lauren? Why do you think we could never be friends?'

She frowned. Did he really need to ask that question? Had he really put the past completely out of his mind? 'I would have thought that was obvious. There's been too much between us for us to ever feel comfortable around each other.'

He shook his head. 'I feel very comfortable around you, Laurie. What you're really saying is that you still blame me for——'

'No, Cole.' Her voice rose, panic very clearly evident now. She didn't want to get into this discussion; this was something she was desperately trying to forget.

'I thought that we might be able to talk about it now. Six months is long enough; we should——'

'Should what?' Her blue eyes shimmered with bitterness. 'Put our ghosts to rest—is that what you are going to say?'

A terrible silence lingered in the room. Cole stared at her, his features granite-hard, only the steady beat of a pulse in the strong line of his neck betraying any emotion. 'No, Lauren,' he murmured, 'I was *not* about to say something that insensitive.'

'You do surprise me.' Her voice was heavy with bitterness.

The dark eyes narrowed and an air of grim resolve seemed to circle around his tall, powerful figure, making his presence oppressively felt in the room. 'Whatever you may think, Lauren, I am genuinely sorry about the baby.'

Silence met that remark. He just continued to stand there, looking gravely down at her. She could feel a sob of anguish rise in her throat and she tried desperately to swallow it down.

'You still don't believe me, do you?'

She swallowed hard. 'Does it matter what I believe?' she asked in a low, raw tone.

'It matters to me,' he answered quietly.

'It's a bit late for guilt, Cole.' She flinched at the look of anger that crossed his face. She shouldn't have said that. Talking like this about the past was like crossing a minefield, and they had just stepped on one big explosive. 'Look, I'm here to work; let's just forget everything else.' She made to turn away from him but he caught her arm in a grip so tight it brought tears to her eyes.

'Not so fast, honey,' he drawled in a voice that made her shiver with fear. 'You don't hurl accusations like that around and then just walk away.'

'I haven't accused you of anything,' she denied breathlessly.

'You said that I feel guilty about something; now to my ears that sounds as if you've attached some liability to me,' he grated harshly. 'And I'm just about sick of taking the rap for something that wasn't my fault.'

Something inside her just seemed to snap at those words. 'You were the one who got me pregnant, Cole, and you were the one who told me you didn't want our baby; somehow I don't think that makes you entirely blameless, does it?' She hurled the words at him with the full force of her bitterness and hurt wedged solidly behind them. 'Now why don't you go back to Donna, where you belong?'

CHAPTER TWO

THE words hung in the stillness of the room. As soon as they were spoken Lauren wished with all her heart that she could call them back. So much for being unemotional and professional. The good intentions had lasted all of ten minutes.

Cole let go of her arm. She flicked an uncertain glance up at him. His features were closed, withdrawn, and she couldn't tell if he was angry or just plain bored by the emotional outburst.

She rubbed absently at her arm, which was still throbbing from the pressure of his grip. 'Cole, I'm sorry.' She shrugged despondently. 'I shouldn't have said that.'

'No,' he agreed in a heavy tone.

Her heart thudded nervously. Was he about to tell her to pack up her things and return to London? She would refuse, of course, but following him furtively for news of his impending wedding wasn't the kind of story Warren was expecting. 'Look, if you want the *Record* to send another reporter——'

'No, Lauren, that's not what I want,' he grated, and there was an edge to his voice that she didn't understand.

Before she had time to say anything else they were interrupted by a knock on the door. 'Lauren, honey, are you ready to go down for dinner?' It was Jon's good-humoured tone.

Cole's eyes met hers. 'You haven't wasted much time finding yourself an escort for the evening, have you?' he murmured sardonically.

She slanted a defiant look up at him. 'That,' she told him firmly, 'is the photographic journalist who has accompanied me.'

The firm mouth tightened imperceptibly. The dark eyes that stared down at her had an ominous look about them. Strange how Cole didn't have to say anything to denote his displeasure. There was an aura of power that surrounded him, making it possible for him to strike fear into a person's soul with just a glance. He was the type of man nobody in their right mind would want to cross.

'I know you stipulated that you didn't want a photographer,' Lauren went on hastily. 'But Jon and I are a team and we work well together. I want him here.'

'Lauren?' There was another tap on the door. 'Are you all right, honey?' The door opened slightly and Jon Richards put his head tentatively around it.

Jon was a good-looking man, probably just a couple of years younger than Cole's thirty-four years. Dark, intelligent eyes widened slightly as they met with Cole's. 'Sorry, Lauren,' he murmured quickly. 'I thought you were alone.'

'That's all right, Jon. Come in.' Lauren moved over towards him, more than a little grateful for the interruption. 'You're just in time to meet Cole Adams.'

'So I see.' Jon stepped inside. His gaze moved perceptively over Lauren's pale face before moving on to the stern-looking man opposite.

'Cole, this is my friend and colleague, Jon Richards,' Lauren introduced them hastily.

'Pleased to meet you.' With a friendly smile Jon proffered his hand. For one awful moment Lauren thought that Cole was just going to ignore the younger man completely; he made no attempt to take the outstretched hand. Instead his gaze was coolly assessing. 'You know of course that I specifically requested that there be no photographs,' he drawled lazily after a strained moment of silence.

'Well—er—yes.' Jon dropped his hand, and then raked it in an embarrassed, self-conscious way through thick blond hair as he stole an uncertain glance at Lauren. 'Lauren rather hoped that she could persuade you otherwise.'

'Did she, now?' Cole shot a look at her and his displeasure seemed to have changed to amusement. 'And how were you planning to persuade me, Laurie?' There was something intensely personal about the way he asked that question. Lauren could feel her face flooding with warm colour. His words and the way he asked that question conjured up memories of the past, memories that were disturbingly intense.

The firm mouth slanted in a half-smile. 'Never mind,' he murmured. 'You can surprise me. If I remember rightly you were very...imaginative and highly successful once before when you tried to win me over regarding an interview.'

Her face was on fire now. How could he be so insensitive as to make jokes about that episode? At this moment she hated Cole with an intensity that hurt.

He glanced at his watch. 'Well, I'll leave you.' His mood was dismissive now. His eyes flicked over them both and then rested on Jon. 'We have two or three days' work left on the video we're currently shooting. You're welcome to come along and take a few photos while we work. We start at five-thirty tomorrow with some shots taken out at the Grand Palace.'

'That would be great!' Jon's eyes brightened.

Cole nodded. 'That's all I'm offering you. Once work is finished I don't want a photographer within a hundred miles of me. Is that understood?'

'Unless Lauren persuades you otherwise.' Jon grinned. 'I know from past experience that she usually gets what she wants.'

Cole did not look amused. His eyes were hard and calculating as they rested on Lauren. 'That makes two of us,' he said drily. Then he turned towards the door. 'By the way, the crew I'm working with know nothing of my wedding plans. I'd like it to stay that way.' He slanted a look back at them, a look that was definitely not to be argued with. 'Have I made myself clear?'

'As crystal,' Lauren murmured, a dry edge to her voice.

'Good, because if you breach that confidence there will be no story, no interview.' The door opened then closed behind him with a quiet finality that was strangely chilling.

'Whew...' Jon let out a long breath. 'That guy is something else. Tough, unapproachable and yet there is something about him...you can't help feeling a grudging respect.'

Lauren didn't answer. She was waging a strange war within herself. Seeing Cole again had stirred up so many mixed emotions, so many memories. Pride and passion had been kicked and battered around inside her so much where that man was concerned, and it still hurt like hell. She had known that seeing him again would be difficult, but she hadn't been prepared for how much it would still hurt.

'Lauren?' Jon's voice cut into her thoughts. 'You haven't heard a word I've just said, have you?' he asked with a rueful grin.

She grimaced. 'Sorry, Jon, I was miles away.'

'Do you still love him?'

The quietly asked question lingered in the stillness of the room, taking her very much by surprise. Clear blue eyes stared at the handsome face and dark eyes that were watching her so closely. 'What kind of a stupid question is that?' she breathed angrily.

He smiled. 'The kind a man asks when he notices the woman he happens to be very fond of looking as if she has been punched in the solar plexus.'

Soft lips twisted ruefully. 'I suppose, if I'm going to be truthful about it, I'm finding this assignment very difficult.'

'Understandably so.' Jon moved towards the mini bar in the room and helped himself to a drink. 'Want one?'

About to refuse, she changed her mind. 'A gin and tonic would be nice.' She moved across the room and sat down at the table next to the sliding glass windows. A quiet drink might help to ease the tension invading her body.

'You were with Adams quite a while. It will be hard for you seeing him with someone else,' Jon continued as he came over to join her.

'No, I really don't care that he has someone special now; in fact I'm happy for him.' She took the drink he passed over and nursed it, a look of determination on her young face. She would never allow Cole Adams to upset her again; she had shed her last tear over that man.

'If you say so.' Jon didn't sound convinced. 'But if you need a shoulder, you know where I am.'

'Thanks, Jon, but I'm well over Cole Adams,' she said briskly.

He shrugged. 'Well, the offer is there if you need it.' Dark eyes moved over the delicate beauty of her face. 'All I can say is, the man is crazy.'

There was just something a little too intimate about the remark, about the look in his eyes. For a moment Lauren felt uncomfortable. She hoped Jon wasn't entertaining any romantic ideas about her. She knew he had the reputation around the office for being a bit of a philanderer, but he had never made a pass at her, and quite frankly that was the last thing she wanted. Complications of that kind would just spoil a good working relationship.

'Shall we go down and have some dinner?' Jon asked, lightly now. 'Or would you prefer to have room service send something up?'

'Let's go down,' Lauren said. She finished her drink and stood up. 'Come on, then. Just to prove to you that I'm not hiding in my room from our illustrious Mr Adams.'

He got up with a grin. 'Wouldn't have blamed you if you were. Between you, me and the gatepost I found the man a bit intimidating myself. He's not the average pop star type, is he?'

'How do you mean?' They moved together towards the door, Lauren picking up the door-key before they went out into the long silent corridors.

'Well, you know, the jeans and T-shirt, the earring and designer stubble—there's none of that. Adams looks as if he would be more at home in a high-level boardroom; he has the steel-like personality to match a top businessman, not an artist.'

Lauren grinned. 'Cole does spend a lot of time in boardrooms. He owns three of the top record labels now and he has some other very successful business interests.' They stopped by the lifts and she pushed the ground-floor button. 'He does wear jeans—looks good in them too,' she added before she could stop herself. She grinned ruefully at him. 'Yes, I am still a fan. If you had ever seen Cole in concert you would know why; not only does he have a voice like velvet, there's something magnetic about him.'

'He has sex appeal, you mean?' Jon laughed.

Lauren shrugged. She could hardly deny that. Women of all ages seemed to go crazy over Cole. Living with him had brought that fact home very clearly.

The lift arrived, and as they stepped in and the doors closed Lauren closed out the memories that had started to plague her.

The restaurant was practically empty. It had a delightful, tranquil ambience. Candle-light gleamed on the silver set on linen; through sliding glass doors the terrace was lit up and a few couples were dining outside.

'Do you want to sit outside? Or is it too warm for you out there?' Jon asked.

She smiled at him. 'After the icy cold of the London nights it will be a treat to sit outside.'

A waiter led them to a table at the edge of the terrace which looked out over the river. Lauren stared out over the dark expanse of water. A pagoda-shaped building on the other side was lit with brightly coloured lights that reflected in the stillness of the water. 'It's so beautiful and peaceful here,' Lauren said dreamily. 'Makes me wish I was here on holiday, not working.'

'Wait until you get stuck in one of Bangkok's doomsday traffic jams,' Jon grinned. 'You won't think it's so peaceful then.'

The waiter came and took their order and poured them both some iced water.

'It is very beautiful, though,' Jon continued as he left. 'Wait until you see the Grand Palace tomorrow—it will blow your mind. I think Thailand is one of the most romantic destinations I've ever visited. No wonder Cole has chosen to get married out here.'

Lauren made no reply to that. She reached for her glass and took a long drink of the cool water.

'Who do you think is his prospective bride?' Jon went on.

'I'd hazard a guess at Donna Wade. She's his backing singer. They've worked closely together for years.' She kept her voice carefully neutral. 'So I suggest when we go out with them tomorrow that you try and get plenty of photos of them together. At least that way if Cole doesn't allow any photographs of the actual ceremony we'll still have some of them out here.'

Jon nodded. 'I intend to get the photographs that matter, though,' he told her determinedly. 'Even if it means skulking after them through the jungle.'

Lauren had to laugh at that.

Jon grinned at her, then leaned over and lifted her slender hand to his lips in a tender gesture. She frowned at him. 'What was that for?'

'Because I like to see you laughing,' he replied seriously, his dark eyes locking on hers. 'It was also for Adams's benefit. Don't turn around, but he's standing in the doorway behind and if looks could kill I'd be stone dead by now.'

Feeling suddenly uncomfortable, Lauren made to pull her hand away from his. 'No, don't,' Jon said softly. His eyes held hers steadily for a moment. 'Kiss me,' he whispered softly.

'What?' She was totally perplexed now. Before she could move he had leaned closer and brushed her lips in a light caress. She pulled away from him. 'Jon, have you gone quite mad?'

'No.' He grinned at her. 'I thought it would be a good idea to remind Adams of what he's missing.'

'Jon, I——'

'Wow!' Her colleague's low intake of breath interrupted her and she glanced around to see what had caused his sudden interest.

Her heart gave a sick lurch as she saw the woman who was walking over towards Cole. She moved with a swinging, sexy gait. She wore a tight mini-skirt that showed long slim legs that seemed to reach up to her armpits. Glossy long dark hair swung over tanned bare shoulders as she reached up for Cole to kiss her.

'Who is that?' Jon asked, a gleam of masculine interest in his dark eyes.

Lauren's lips twisted in a dry smile. 'That is Donna Wade,' she informed him wryly. 'Now you know why Cole is certainly not missing me. So no more stunts like that kiss, please.'

Jon grimaced at her. 'Spoilsport.' He glanced over at the other couple again. 'Looks as if they're heading over here.'

Lauren felt her heart thud nervously; she didn't feel ready to confront the couple. For some reason even the thought of making polite conversation with them was making her stomach churn.

'Good evening.' Jon stood up politely as the pair reached their table. Lauren turned her head nonchalantly up and her eyes clashed with Donna's sea-green gaze.

'Lauren. How nice to see you again.' The words held only the merest hint of coolness. Donna had never liked Lauren.

'How are you, Donna?' Lauren swallowed down the feelings of resentment towards the other woman. She could hardly blame her for not liking her. Donna had worked for Cole for almost five years now and she had worn her heart on her sleeve for him for all that time. When Lauren had arrived on the scene it couldn't have been easy for her. Anyway, that was all in the past, and she had her man safely in her grasp now. As Lauren was no longer a threat to her, maybe she would be an easier person to know.

'I'm fine, Lauren, except for this terrible heat.' She rolled green eyes upwards. 'Almost eight in the evening and it's still unbearable.'

'I find it quite pleasant,' Lauren remarked idly. She noticed how close Donna was standing to Cole as if they were joined at the hip, her slender body moulded against his tall, powerful frame. She slid a glance upwards towards him, then promptly wished she hadn't as her eyes locked with his deep gaze.

'Well, I suppose it's a treat for you after the cold of London,' Donna continued smoothly. 'Cole and I have just finished an extensive tour of Australia. We're a little bored with the heat now.' She turned provocative green eyes up towards him. 'Aren't we, darling?'

Cole's firm lips slanted in amusement. 'I wouldn't say I was bored, Donna. I haven't really had time for that particular luxury.' His eyes never moved from Lauren's face. 'I'm sure you remember just how hectic being on tour is, Lauren. There's no time for anything.'

Lauren felt her hands curl into tight balls. She didn't want him to talk about things from the past. She didn't want to be reminded of anything.

'Er—would you like to join us?' Jon put in now.

Lauren noticed with annoyance that Cole had already pulled out a chair opposite and had every intention of sitting down, invited or not.

'I don't think I introduced you to Donna, Jon.' Lauren hastily remembered her manners as the other woman sank down gracefully next to Cole.

'Pleased to meet you.' Jon's polite tone met with a cool nod from the brunette.

'I'm sure Lauren remembers being on tour with us very clearly,' Donna continued the conversation from before as if there had been no interruptions, her voice holding a brittle edge. 'You didn't really enjoy it, did you, Lauren? I think that was because you weren't part of the team.'

'Oh, I don't know,' Cole put in lazily. 'I think she was; she did some very good write-ups for us.'

'Yes, but she was bored, Cole,' Donna continued airily. 'Music isn't Lauren's life the way it is ours. You and I thrive on it just as Lauren thrives on getting a good story for her paper. I'm right, aren't I, Lauren?' Sharp green eyes demanded she agree.

'Yes, I suppose you are,' Lauren conceded in a low tone. Anger was bubbling inside. Did the woman really have to go through all this? And did she have to talk about her as if she were some halfwit who wasn't there? She didn't want to have this conversation; she didn't need to be reminded how wrong Cole was for her. She could remember that all too clearly.

She met Cole's dark gaze across the table and her hands tightened unconsciously into tight fists as they rested on the table.

'Well, I enjoyed Lauren's time with us last year,' he said gently. 'I thought she fitted in quite well.'

He was adding insult to injury now by being kind, and Lauren could feel a lump rising in her throat. 'Yes, but Donna is quite right,' she told him drily. 'Journalism is my first love and I did miss it.'

'She's damn good at her job, too.' Jon spoke up for the first time. 'Warren was very glad to have her back at work and of course so was I.' He placed a hand over hers as it rested on the table and squeezed it warmly.

Lauren could feel a flood of angry heat rising under her skin. She didn't care for Jon's patronising tone and she didn't like the way he was now holding her hand. She pulled it away calmly, conscious of the fact that Cole was watching.

'Well, thanks for the vote of confidence, Jon. Speaking of work——' She met Cole's eyes firmly and directly. 'Seeing as we're all sitting here, how about running through a few questions for our article?'

'Sorry, Lauren, but Donna and I are about to go out on the town,' Cole replied smoothly in a tone that wasn't to be argued with. 'I thought it would be a good idea if you and Jon joined us.'

Lauren didn't think that was a good idea at all. In fact it was totally abhorrent. The very notion of going out with the couple while they sat and looked into each other's eyes made her stomach turn.

'Thank you for the invitation, but not tonight, Cole.' Her voice was very carefully controlled and bland as if she were talking to a complete stranger. 'I feel as if I need an early night after our journey today.'

'Of course you do.' Donna stood briskly to her feet. 'You and Jon have a nice relaxing evening together and we'll see you tomorrow.'

Lauren didn't particularly care for the implication that there was something between her and Jon, but she smiled sweetly. 'Thank you. I hope you enjoy your evening out.'

'I'm sure we will,' Cole put in as he got to his feet. 'Remember that we set off early in the morning, Lauren,' he said briskly, his eyes cold as they lingered on her and Jon. 'I won't have anyone disrupting my schedule.'

'We have no intention of disrupting your schedule,' Lauren told him, a gleam of anger in her blue eyes.

'Good, let's keep it like that.'

Before Lauren had a chance to make any reply to that he had placed a guiding hand at Donna's back and the two of them walked away.

Lauren's eyes followed them angrily. How did that man manage to infuriate her out of all proportion with just a mere sentence or two?

She watched them cross the terrace and go down some steps to where a motor launch was waiting on the water.

Cole got into the boat first and then turned to help Donna. His hands went firmly around her tiny waist as he swung her safely down beside him. For a moment she clung to him, looking slender and incredibly feminine beside his tall, broad-shouldered frame. Then he moved away from her and started up the engine of the boat. A few seconds later they were speeding out across the river.

Lauren looked away from them and forced a smile to her lips as she met Jon's gaze. 'They're made for each other, don't you think?' she said in a brittle tone.

He shrugged. 'Donna is certainly extremely beautiful.'

'Yes, beautiful and in perfect tune with his way of life. What more could a man want?'

Lauren couldn't sleep that night. She tried to tell herself it was because her body clock was not properly adjusted to the time change from London, nothing to do with seeing Cole again. He meant nothing to her now. In her mind's eye she saw Donna and him out on the terrace again, saw the way they had stood so close together, the way he had held her close as he helped her on to the motor launch.

She tossed restlessly on the bed and then got up to switch up the air-conditioning. It was a combination of heat and jet lag that was making her dwell so much on that incident. Would Donna be with him now? The question sprang unwanted into her mind. She glanced at the clock beside her bed. Half-three in the morning—of course they would be together, curled up in some large double bed, arms entwined sensuously. Lauren swallowed hard, her mouth suddenly dry.

She moved to pour herself some iced water, then lay back down on the bed, switching the lights off. Darkness closed in around her, and with it unwanted memories.

There was a rumour flying around that Cole Adams was buying one of the largest record companies, TDR. 'Get me the inside story, Lauren, and there's a big promotion for you,' her editor had told her nonchalantly. It was like dangling a huge chocolate cake tantalisingly out of reach of a chocolate addict. Lauren had been working for the *Global Record* newspaper for a year and she had poured her heart and soul into the job. There had been no time in her life for romance or socialising; all her energy was going into her career. The prospect of getting some well-deserved recognition was like manna from heaven.

The only problem was, Cole Adams did not give interviews. He was the type of man who liked to keep his personal life completely private. Most of the articles that had been written about the star had been based on pure supposition.

She tried calling his home, and got his secretary, who told her categorically that Mr Adams would not see her. She didn't leave it there; she phoned several times. Once she even got Cole; it must have been a sheer fluke because he never seemed to answer his own phone. She knew it was him immediately—that husky, attractive drawl could not belong to anyone else. He didn't even hear her out; once she mentioned the *Global Record* the phone was swiftly put down on her.

It was totally frustrating. All it would cost him was ten, maybe fifteen minutes of his time, and it would make all the difference to her whole career.

She hung around outside the huge wrought-iron gates to his London house but she never even caught a glimpse of his black limousine.

She tried to research his movements, no easy task where Cole Adams was concerned. The man seemed to be shrouded in mystery. Then she came across a very interesting bit of information. He was on the board of a big children's charity organisation and he met at regular periods with its chairman, Edward Carter. She had done an article on that man a few months ago and the one thing she remembered very clearly about him was the fact that he had been completely infatuated by her. In fact from time to time he still rang her to ask her out for dinner. That evening she found his number and called him.

It took two outings to dinner and one trip to the theatre before she nonchalantly broached the subject of Cole Adams, just saying that she was a big fan.

Edward was delighted to be able to tell her that he knew the man well, that he was meeting him for lunch next week in fact.

'Really?' Lauren looked suitably impressed and batted wide blue eyes. 'I'd give anything to meet him,' she had drawled wistfully.

Edward had been silent for a moment. 'Well, I'd invite you along, but I know for a fact that Cole has an aversion to members of the Press, and we are only meeting to discuss business——'

'Oh, Edward! Do you really think you could invite me along? We needn't tell him I'm a journalist; I'll sit as quiet as a little mouse.' She reached across and kissed his cheek, blue eyes brimming over with excitement and gratitude. 'Anything you discuss with him will be completely confidential; you needn't worry about my being there.'

Lauren had meant what she said, she would never have compromised Edward by repeating any of the business that was discussed at that table. Her goal had been to establish contact with Cole and take it from there.

Nevertheless she had felt incredibly guilty when she had achieved what she had wanted with such relative ease. Edward was a nice guy, early thirties, unassuming, which was surprising considering he was incredibly wealthy. He was obviously crazy about her and she was unashamedly using him. Had her career become so important that it had overtaken common decency?

It wasn't the time for introspective doubts. They were sitting in the stylish French restaurant, Le Rendezvous, which was a favourite meeting place for the rich and famous, and Cole's arrival was imminent. She had glanced across at Edward's pleasant good-humoured face and had swallowed down her pangs of conscience. A good journalist had to make use of contacts every now and then.

'Here he is,' Edward murmured, and her eyes swung out across the crowded restaurant and locked on the powerfully attractive man who was crossing towards them. Cole had quite literally taken her breath away. She had seen him before of course, on the television and in the papers. She knew he was a good-looking man, a man women adored, but she had been completely unprepared for the impact he had on her.

Heads turned as he walked past and he stopped now and then to have a quiet word with one or two eminent people. Then he was standing by their table and Edward was rising to his feet.

'Nice to see you again, Cole.' He stretched out his hand and it was taken in a firm handshake.

Edward was a tall, well-built man yet next to Cole he looked almost feeble. Cole was easily a head taller; his body was taut and superbly fit. The dark suit he wore emphasised the power of his broad shoulders, the white silk shirt, the rugged, healthy tan.

'I'd like you to meet my girlfriend, Lauren Martin.' Edward introduced her with a note of pride in his voice.

Dark eyes looked down at her, and held her long and hard. The strangest sensation filled her body. She felt as if she were skiing at full speed down an icy mountain only to run full pelt into a warm embrace. An embrace that made her want to melt with pleasure. 'Miss Martin.' He acknowledged her with the merest nod of his head, then his eyes released her.

He sat in the seat directly facing her. Edward was gabbling on, nervously so, Lauren thought. Cole obviously had an unnerving influence on him also. Cole listened to every word, an aura of strength and authority seeming to prevail through his silence.

The waiter arrived for their order and Lauren realised that she had forgotten to study the menu, so engrossed had she been in the man opposite. She chose hastily and then watched Cole as he studied the wine list.

'Any preferences?' The dark eyes rested briefly on Lauren first before moving to Edward.

He shrugged. 'We'll leave it to you.' His eyes darted nervously to Lauren. 'If that's all right with you, honey?'

She nodded, and as she glanced back at Cole their eyes collided. He was studying her lazily from the tip of her blonde gleaming hair down over the blue jacket of her suit which emphasised her curvy figure. She could feel herself growing hot under his scrutiny. It was the first time in her life that a man's mere gaze had made her so acutely conscious of her own body that her heart had quite literally gone into a state of palpitation. She looked away from him hastily.

What on earth was the matter with her? She should be taking control of this situation now. She had prepared her strategy very carefully beforehand; she should be in Phase One of her plan by now, Phase One being a little gentle flirting with the man. Her nerves went into complete turmoil at the very idea. She could never flirt with this man; every instinct was warning her very loudly that to do so spelt danger with a capital 'D'.

Luncheon progressed at a leisurely pace. Edward, discussing business, seemed totally unaware of any undercurrents at the table. Yet to Lauren the air was crackling with some kind of tension. She said very little, only speaking when Edward directed a comment towards her from time to time. Cole did not speak directly to her at all until he had cleared the points of business he had come to discuss.

The dishes from their main course were being cleared away when he turned and suddenly addressed her. 'What do you do for a living, Lauren?' he asked casually. His face was taut as he waited for her reply, yet there was a suggestion of humour in the dark eyes. Almost as if for some reason he found her amusing.

'I'm a writer.' She forced herself to meet those eyes steadily.

'Really,' he drawled. 'And what do you write, fact or fiction?'

Lauren frowned; was there an undercurrent of mockery in that question or was she just going completely paranoid where this man was concerned? 'A little of both.' Her answer was deliberately non-committal. She was definitely not about to reveal the fact that she was a journalist.

A waiter interrupted the conversation. 'Excuse me, Mr Carter, there's a telephone call for you.'

Edward frowned. 'Can I take it at the table?'

'No, sir, I'm afraid the telephone is out in the bar area.'

With a sigh Edward got to his feet. 'Sorry about this, I won't be long,' he murmured to them, and followed the waiter out across the room.

Lauren's nerves tingled. She had deliberately arranged for a colleague to place that call so that she would be left alone with Cole for a few minutes. She had hoped that they would be sufficiently relaxed by now that she could ask a few discreet questions.

She glanced across at him and as their eyes met her mind went into a kind of blank paralysis. Silence stretched for a moment. Then he glanced lazily at his watch.

'So,' he drawled in a indolent tone. 'Aren't you wasting time?'

'Sorry?' Puzzled cornflower-blue eyes searched the rugged features, unsure of what he was talking about.

'You've obviously gone to a lot of trouble to arrange this meeting, Miss Martin,' he said in a dry voice. 'And now that you have successfully got me on my own, I am waiting for you to ask the questions that you have obviously been burning to ask me for weeks.'

Lauren fought hard not to allow her mouth to drop open. 'You know?' she managed at last in an incredulous tone.

'Of course I know,' he said disdainfully. 'My security cameras at the gates of my house have been trained on you for almost three weeks.'

'Oh!' Lauren felt incredibly foolish now. She hadn't seen any cameras when she had waited outside his residence.

'Oh, indeed.' He leaned back in his chair and studied her idly. 'So how far did you have to go with Carter to get an invite here today?' he drawled sardonically.

Lauren stared coldly at him; she didn't like the implied suggestion in that question. 'Edward invited me here today as a friend.'

Cole gave a short dry laugh. 'Well, the poor fool is infatuated with you, that's for sure. I take it, then, that he doesn't know he is being manipulated by you.'

'I have not manipulated him, I've——'

'Merely used him,' Cole finished for her drily. 'My God, you people really have no scruples, have you?' he said disdainfully. 'Carter happens to be a nice guy; have you ever stopped to think that the games you are playing with him could hurt?'

'I am not playing games,' she told him coolly. 'I'm trying to earn my living. All I want is a few minutes of your time.'

He flicked another glance at his gold wristwatch. 'You've already wasted five minutes of it. And by the look of it Carter is just about to rejoin us.'

Lauren's spirits sank as she looked across the restaurant and saw Edward talking to the waiter. 'Damn,' she muttered under her breath.

One dark eyebrow lifted in sardonic amusement. 'Looks as if you've blown it, doesn't it?'

'Yes.' She sat back in her chair and her blue eyes shimmered with resentment as she looked over at him. 'What's it like to have the power to make or break someone's career, Mr Adams?'

He didn't answer her immediately; his dark eyes were raking over the pallor of her skin, the vulnerable curve of her lips.

'Ten minutes of your time and I would have had the promotion I've been working towards for twelve months,' she went on in a low tone.

'And you want that promotion pretty badly, don't you?' he said thoughtfully.

She held her breath at that note in his voice, a glimmer of hope in her blue eyes as she nodded her head.

He pursed his lips and for a moment there was silence. She tried to ignore the way his eyes moved in a hard, assessing way over her. Then he shrugged. 'What the hell? Get yourself out to my house at nine this evening and we'll take it from there.'

Elation mixed with apprehension inside Lauren at those words. What did he mean by 'take it from there'? There was no time to ask, because Edward joined them again at that moment.

The waiter brought their coffee and Lauren sipped at it, trying to look nonchalant, trying not to look as if her mind and her body were in complete turmoil.

There was something about Cole Adams that completely overturned the businesslike cool that always surrounded Lauren. No man had ever made her whole body tingle just by looking at her; no man had ever made her forget the important questions she had come to ask.

When she had presented herself at Cole's house later that evening she had been more than a little nervous. Why she should feel like that was beyond her. She had interviewed lots of famous people, lots of handsome men. What was it about Cole Adams that made her nerves tingle, that made her acutely conscious of herself as a woman first and then a journalist?

She had never before been in an agony of indecision over what to wear when interviewing a subject, yet for Cole she went through her wardrobe very carefully and selected a red suit that was businesslike yet feminine. It stopped just above the knee, showing her shapely long legs to their best advantage, and the double-breasted jacket with its brass buttons gave a wonderful emphasis to her narrow waist and curving figure.

His house was a surprise; she had expected an ultra-modern décor. Instead it was tastefully furnished with beautiful antiques and *objets d'art* that had been collected from different corners of the world, all priceless, all of breathtaking beauty.

'It's a hobby of mine,' Cole informed her when he joined her in his living-room and found her admiring an exquisite Ming vase. 'When I go on tour I always set aside some time to go searching for something new to add to my collection. I can't resist things of great beauty; I just have to have them.'

Something about the way he said those words, and the way his dark eyes were moving over her, made her blush.

He smiled, that lazy, heart-stopping smile that made her pulses race. 'Sit down, please.' He waved her towards the deep sofa with its Chinese embroidered covers of exotic birds and flowers.

She sat, carefully pulling the straight skirt so that it was covering as much of her legs as possible.

'What can I get you to drink?' He moved towards the drinks cabinet and poured himself a Scotch.

He was wearing the same dark suit he had been wearing at lunch and he looked magnificent. Lauren wished suddenly that she hadn't bothered to change; it looked as if she had made a special effort just to impress him, and he was just so laid-back that it made her feel silly.

'I don't drink when I'm working, thank you,' she said primly, taking her notebook, pen and small recorder out of her handbag.

One dark eyebrow rose in a rather mocking way. 'I don't think we should start work straight away,' he drawled. 'I think we should get to know each other a little better first.'

She crossed her legs and glanced away from him nervously. She didn't say anything; she didn't really know what to say. She didn't think she was handling this very well, didn't feel in control of proceedings.

'Let's see.' He paused thoughtfully with his hand over a row of crystal glasses. 'Yes, I think you would probably like a white wine and soda; am I right?'

She shrugged. 'Anything will be fine.'

He brought their drinks across and sat next to her on the settee. She had to force herself not to move away. His closeness was unnerving her.

He turned sideways to face her and leaned back lazily against the cushions. 'So, Lauren.' His voice lingered softly over her name almost as if he were tasting it on his lips. 'Tell me a little about yourself.'

Her hands tightened around the cold crystal glass. 'I'm supposed to be interviewing you, remember?' she jested lightly.

He smiled. 'Well, humour me. You talk a little about yourself and we'll get into a nice relaxed mood and then get to me. How does that sound?'

She shrugged. 'It sounds different,' she admitted huskily. 'It's not how I usually conduct an interview.'

'Well, I like to be different.' He grinned. 'So, where do you live and who do you live with?'

She took a hasty sip of her drink. 'I live alone in my flat in St John's Wood. I...I just rent it. It belongs to my parents but they live in Spain now. I'm twenty-three and I'm dedicated to my career, which I love.' She shrugged self-consciously. 'There, that's all there is to know.'

'Oh, I don't think so,' he said in a dangerously gentle tone. 'I think that beneath that icy reserve of yours there are sensuous fires just waiting to be discovered.'

She put her drink down on the table beside them, her hand none too steady. 'That's nonsense, Mr Adams.' The businesslike cool of her voice held a faint tremor. 'I'm a journalist, I have come to do a job. There is nothing deeper than that going on beneath my surface. What you see is what you get.'

'Really?' One eyebrow lifted and his dark eyes were filled with amusement. 'That sounds hopeful.'

She picked up her notebook with trembling hands, trying to ignore the innuendo and wishing with all her heart that she hadn't said that. 'So, can you tell me if there is any truth in the rumour that you have just bought the large record label TDR?' she enquired crisply.

'Well——' he took a sip of his whisky and put it down '—let's just say that there's no smoke without fire.' The dark eyes looked at her steadily, taking in every detail of her appearance.

Heat started to rise under her creamy skin and he smiled and then reached for her.

The touch of his hands on her shoulders sent her heart into overdrive. 'Now, let's see,' he went on in a husky tone. 'I'm thirty-four. Single. Two houses—this one and a ranch in California.' His hand moved gently to cup her chin, and the touch of his skin against hers sent a shiver of ecstasy racing through her. 'And I like to collect beautiful objects of rare and exciting excellence,' he breathed softly, his face coming steadily nearer.

China-blue eyes held with his. 'I am not a collectable object,' she told him in a tone that was barely a whisper.

'I beg to differ there.' He smiled and his lips brushed against hers with teasing, delectable warmth. 'You have to be my most exciting find ever.'

Cole had literally swept her away on a tide of emotion. He had broken all the rules she made for herself and all the barriers that surrounded her.

Within a week of meeting him, she had given up the job that had been her most prized and coveted possession, so in that respect she supposed she had given up everything just to be with him while he worked on a world tour.

At the time it had not been a hard sacrifice to make. But then she had never imagined for one moment that she was giving everything up for a relationship that had no future, and that one day she would be interviewing him about his forthcoming marriage to another woman.

CHAPTER THREE

A LOUD knocking awoke Lauren. For a moment she stared up at the unfamiliar ceiling and wondered where she was. She felt awful, her head was pounding as if she had been drinking heavily the night before. She frowned and sat up slowly.

The hotel bedroom was bathed in early morning sunlight. She closed her eyes to the golden brightness and reached blindly for her silk wrap that was sitting on the chair beside her.

'Lauren, are you up?' It was Jon's voice coming from outside the door.

'I'm coming.' She hurriedly moved to let him in, her head thudding at the noise.

'And how are you this morning?' Jon breezed in, looking very bright for so early in the morning.

'Fine.' Defiantly she blocked out the fact that tormented memories of Cole had kept her awake for half the night and forced a cheerful smile to her lips. 'Ring down to Reception, and see if they'll send up some coffee, will you, Jon?' she said, walking towards the wardrobe.

'Sure thing.' Jon sat on the edge of her bed and reached for the phone. When he had finished talking he sat back against the headboard and put his feet up. 'This is rather an ungodly time to begin work,' he murmured lazily. 'I could use some caffeine myself.'

Lauren wasn't really listening; her eyes were moving over the few outfits that were hung up inside the wardrobe.

'Put something long on,' Jon told her helpfully. 'I meant to tell you that last night. The Thai people like you to dress modestly as a mark of respect when you visit the Grand Palace.'

A knock at the door interrupted their conversation. 'That was quick!' Lauren said in surprise. Thinking it was their coffee, she called for them to come in.

The door opened, but it wasn't a member of staff who came in—it was Cole. Dark eyes moved over her slender figure in the white silk nightwear. She could feel her colour rising in her cheeks as his glance went slowly from the tip of her toes up over her body to rest on her face. His eyes held hers for a moment before his gaze transferred to Jon, who was still reclining lazily on the bed.

'We leave in fifteen minutes,' he informed them coolly. 'If you're not down by then, we will presume you are not coming.'

'Of course we're coming,' Lauren put in firmly.

His eyes swivelled back to her, cold and hard. She couldn't help comparing that look with the way he used to look at her. It didn't take long for passion to die, she thought sadly. There had been a time when his eyes had lit up when he looked at her. Now there was somebody new in his bed and she was just a hazy memory from the past. There was a tight knot of pain gathering in her chest, like a storm cloud of tears gathering and waiting to explode. She swallowed down the feeling and turned towards the wardrobe.

'I'll be five minutes,' she told him lightly over her shoulder.

'See that you are,' he said curtly, turning to leave. 'I won't wait.'

Lauren's hands stilled on the row of clothes. Those words echoing in the painful recesses of her memory. I won't wait for you. I won't wait, they screamed and screamed over and over again.

The door closed behind him and she closed her eyes as the cloud of tears moved upwards to distort her vision. Those were the last words he had said to her before he had walked out of her life six months ago. He had tossed her an ultimatum and then calmly walked away from her, his conscience cleared.

'I'd better get downstairs.' Jon got hastily up from the bed and picked up his bag of photographic equipment that he had left on the chair.

'Lauren?' He paused in the doorway and she forced herself to pull herself around and face him. His eyes rested thoughtfully on her pale features. 'Do you want me to make it clear to Cole that nothing is going on between us?'

She frowned, the question completely taking her by surprise. 'I don't think Cole is the slightest bit interested in what's going on in my personal life,' she told him without any indecision.

'No?' One blond eyebrow lifted doubtfully. 'I don't think he looked too pleased when he saw me reclining on your bed.'

Her lips twisted in a rueful smile. 'Cole couldn't give a damn about me, Jon. He's about to become a married man, remember? All he's concerned about is his precious schedule. Time is money; he had a whole crew of cameramen and technicians to round up this morning and he won't allow anyone to hold him up, least of all us.'

'Well, if you're sure.' Jon grinned at her. 'I'll see you downstairs, then.'

Exactly ten minutes later Lauren joined him down on the terrace. She wore a long skirt in pastel shades of blue and pink and a cool T-shirt in a matching pink. It was a pretty outfit, practical yet feminine. Her long blonde hair was piled up on top of her head for coolness and she wore the faintest hint of pink on her lips just to add a little colour to the pallor of her skin.

Jon was engaged in an animated conversation with some of the camera crew, who were loading their gear into a boat moored by the landing stage to the terrace. There was no sign of Donna, but Cole was standing checking equipment off on a clipboard as the men picked it up.

A few of the musicians who worked on the instrumentals for Cole's records were sitting finishing their coffee as they waited for the boss to give the word that they were ready to move out. Lauren recognised most of them. She had travelled on tour for nearly a year with Cole so she had got to know the people he worked with pretty well in that time.

'Lauren!' One of them glanced up and caught sight of her and his boyishly attractive face creased into a wealth of smiles. 'It's terrific to see you again,' he enthused with genuine sincerity.

'Hello, Jed.' She smiled a trifle shyly as they all rose to their feet to greet her. 'Boys,' she acknowledged them all.

'Well, this is a real nice surprise.' One of them pulled out a chair for her.

'We sure as hell have missed you,' Jed was saying now. 'Does this mean that you and Cole are getting back together?' He sounded highly delighted at the idea.

Lauren felt herself colouring up with uncomfortable heat. 'No... no, I'm just here to do a story on you all. I thought Cole might have mentioned I was coming out for a short while——'

'Too much excitement is bad for them,' Cole's dry voice interrupted them. 'The boats are ready and waiting, so I suggest we leave.'

'What a slave-driver.' Jed shook his head, but his words held a jovial tone; all the men liked and respected Cole, were always quick to do as he asked. 'Where's

Donna?' he went on to ask. 'We can hardly leave without her.'

'She'll be down any minute,' Cole murmured, glancing at his watch. 'She's not been sleeping too well these last few nights; the heat is getting to her.'

Lauren bit down on the softness of her lower lip. I just bet it is, she thought with uncharacteristic derision.

As if on cue the french doors out on to the terrace opened and Donna came towards them. Every man's head turned to watch her as she moved gracefully, her long hair flowing in a dark, silky curtain around her shoulders, wearing a long red dress designed to cling to the sensuous shape of her body.

Donna had always enjoyed making an entrance, Lauren remembered wryly.

She pushed a slender hand through dark hair and smiled at the men. Her make-up was perfect, emphasising the cat-green eyes and pouting lips.

'Sorry I'm late.' She gave Cole a special smile and he shrugged broad shoulders dismissively.

'Doesn't matter, we're only just ready.'

And of course he would have waited for her, Lauren thought with rancour, seeing as the heat was 'getting to her' at night.

Donna gave Lauren a cool smile and her green eyes ran swiftly over her, taking in every detail of her appearance. 'You don't look too well this morning, Lauren,' she observed drily.

'Really? I feel fine,' Lauren answered brightly. She knew she looked a little pale, but did Donna really have to point out the fact so loudly?

'I'm feeling a little delicate myself,' Donna went on with a smile. 'Cole and I ended up having a late night last night.' She glanced over at Cole with a provocative smile. 'I hope you haven't lined up too much work for me today, darling. It would be very cruel of you.'

'Now, would I work you too hard?' Cole grinned, a teasing light in his eyes. 'Never mind, Donna, we'll soon be lazing on the deserted tropical beaches around Phuket. You'll feel much better once you get in the clear turquoise seas.'

'Mmm.' She smiled up at him. 'I can hardly wait.'

He put an arm around her slender waist and turned her towards the waiting boats. 'Well, the sooner we get started, the sooner we finish.'

Amen to that, Lauren thought drily as she got to her feet. Everyone started to move towards the boats that were moored beside the floating platform off the terrace.

Jon caught up with her as it was her turn to board the motorised launch. 'Did you hear Cole mentioning Phuket?' he murmured casually in a voice close to his ear.

She nodded. 'Do you think that's where the wedding's to take place?'

'Either that or the honeymoon,' Jon grinned. 'This is turning out to be easier than we thought. Looks as if I'm going to get all the pictures I want.'

'I don't know.' Lauren frowned. 'Phuket is one of Thailand's largest islands. They could lose us easily enough if they wanted to.'

'No chance,' Jon said with confidence, raising his camera to take a few photos of Donna and Cole as they stood close together at the stern of the boat. 'Wherever Cole goes, I'm going to be a couple of steps behind.'

The boat pulled out and moved at a steady pace down the wide expanse of water. Even though it was so early in the morning, the river was alive with people going about their business. They passed scows heavily laden with coconuts, large tankers, water-taxis, houseboats and rice-barges. People obviously lived and worked along these banks.

Lauren watched it all in fascination: the luxurious hotels with colourful flowers and fountains, the canals that led off the main stretches of water and teemed with floating markets of vegetables and rice.

A hand rested on her shoulder and she dragged her eyes away from the dazzlingly colourful scenes to see that Cole was standing next to her.

'Beautiful, isn't it?' he murmured.

'Certainly is.' She kept her voice crisp and her eyes averted out to the passing scenery. She wished he would go and stand somewhere else; his closeness was unnerving.

They passed a scow laden with exotic fruits, a young girl who only looked about ten years of age paddling the heavy load steadily. She glanced up as she passed and, catching Cole's eye, gave him the sweetest of smiles.

Lauren couldn't help smiling and slanted a glance up at him. 'You wow the women wherever you go, don't you, Cole?'

'Sometimes.' He lifted one eyebrow in a roguish, teasing manner and met her gaze. 'There was a time when you used to smile at me like that.'

The laughter died in her eyes. 'That seems like a whole lifetime ago. We're both different people now.'

Cole shook his head. 'I haven't changed that much.' The deep eyes searched her pale face. 'I still think you're extremely beautiful.'

For a moment she was held under the spell of those dark eyes. Then he reached up and soothed away a stray curl from the side of her face with a gentle hand that whispered along her soft skin like a caress.

Her heart thundered with chaotic intensity at that touch and she had to force herself to move a step away from him. 'You... you haven't changed, have you?' she murmured with a shake of her head. 'You're about to be married and yet you still find it necessary to flirt. Are you just a compulsive womaniser, Cole, or isn't your intended bride satisfying you?' She flung the question at him with bitter contempt.

His lips twisted wryly. 'Let's just say she's giving me a few unexpected problems.'

Blue eyes glittered with fury. 'Well, I suggest you sort your problems out with her. Just keep away from me, I'm immune to your particular brand of charm and I'm definitely not in the market for any casual fling.'

'Pity.' He drawled the word with dry humour. 'Not mixing business with pleasure any more, hmm? I thought you were going to try and persuade me to let Jon stay on.'

Her face suffused with deep red colour. Anger and humiliation raged through her. 'If you were hoping for a quick roll in the hay, then I'm afraid I'm going to have to disappoint you,' she told him through tightly clenched teeth. 'I'm very particular who I take to my bed these days.'

'You could have fooled me,' he grated harshly, his eyes moving pointedly towards Jon, who was standing very close to Donna on the opposite side of the boat.

Her eyes followed his. 'You've got a very nasty mind, do you know that, Cole?' she told him angrily. 'And for your information, Jon is a sweet and caring man.'

Sardonic eyes swept her features. 'Not a very passionate statement, and if I remember rightly you used to be a very passionate type. Settling for dull nowadays, are you, Lauren?'

'Settling for my career and a relationship that's real.' Her voice shook slightly and she swung away from him before the tenuous hold she had on her emotions slipped. For a moment her hands had itched to slap that infuriatingly arrogant face.

How dared he try it on with her like that? Did he think, because she had once given herself to him without reservation, that she was some easy target for a one-night stand? Her pride and self-respect rebelled furiously against such an idea, and deep down inside there was a hurt that went so deep, it was almost unbearable. She had given herself to Cole because she had mistakenly believed that what they felt for each other was love. That he should think so little of her as to suggest some sordid little liaison... The man had to be the most arrogant, insufferable, cold-blooded swine she had ever met.

She watched as the boat was cleverly manoeuvred in beside a floating platform and tied so that they could disembark.

'Looks as if we were wrong about Donna and Cole escaping off on their own to Phuket.' Jon joined her as everyone started to gather up their belongings and leave the boat. 'Donna has just told me that everyone is flying out there once the filming here is finished. They're shooting the last track of the album out there.'

'Oh.' Lauren's voice sounded as flat as she felt. At this precise moment she couldn't have cared a damn about the assignment or Cole's marriage arrangements.

'You OK?' Jon darted a searching glance at her.

'Fine.' She watched Cole and Donna walking away from the boat. 'Did she mention anything about the wedding?' She forced herself to inject a note of businesslike interest into the conversation.

'Not a word. She's totally engrossed in work at the moment, though. Apparently Cole is allowing her to do a song of her own on this album. They're shooting part of it here and part down at Phuket.'

'Lucky Donna.' She tried to eliminate all traces of bitterness from her tone. After all, she should feel a little sorry for her. Cole would never be a one-woman type of man, and although he probably loved Donna in his own way it looked as if he was not going to give up his roving eye. The way he had just propositioned her was proof of that.

The Grand Palace was like a mystical exotic city enclosed behind a white crenellated wall. Gold spires and red-tiled, steeply sloping roofs towered into the blue sky. Royal, religious and government buildings dazzled the eye with their colour and ornate beauty.

The camera crew had set up their equipment across from the Royal Chapel and Cole was soon busy organising everyone. Every shot the camera crew took seemed to take an eternity. Jon's camera clicked happily as he took photos of Donna then the crew and Cole.

'I never realised shooting a video was such laborious hard work,' Lauren remarked as Jon stopped next to her to change a roll of film.

'Certainly is. Adams is a perfectionist, though, and he is driving them very hard.'

Lauren nodded. 'I feel sorry for them. It can't be much fun working in this heat. I feel tired just standing here.'

Jon's eyes moved with concern over her pale features. 'You should really have a hat on,' he remarked and put up a gently concerned hand to brush away a stray curl from her forehead. 'Why don't you go into the temple behind you? It will be cool inside and it houses the Emerald Buddha, one of Thailand's most venerated religious statues. It's worth seeing, Lauren, and I think Cole is going to be a while yet.'

Lauren smiled gratefully at the thoughtful suggestion. It was probably a very good idea. It did look as if they were going to be here for quite some time.

As she turned away from Jon she caught Cole watching them. There was a stern look about him, and the dark eyes were thoughtful, his mouth set in a firm line.

Then he turned his attention away and back towards Donna. 'No, not like that, Donna, cut...cut.' She could hear his brisk voice directing the camera crew. Lauren moved away and up the steps to the Royal Chapel.

She took her shoes off before entering. It did feel cooler inside away from the intense rays of the sun. Gold and bright jewel colours dazzled her eyes and it was hard to take in all the ornate beauty around her at first glance. She sat on the floor with her feet tucked away behind her and gazed up at the little Emerald Buddha.

She must have lost track of time sitting there, because the next thing she remembered was a firm hand on her shoulder and Cole's whispered voice in the stillness of the room telling her that they were ready to leave.

She followed him outside, blinking in the brightness of the sun.

'It's getting a little too hot for working now.' His voice was crisp and businesslike. 'So we're taking a break for lunch.'

She nodded absently and looked around for the rest of the crew. They were nowhere in sight and neither were Jon and Donna.

'Where is everyone?' She put her hand over her eyes to shadow her face from the sun as she looked up at Cole.

'I told you, they've gone for lunch.' His tone was briskly impatient. 'And I suggest we do the same.'

'What—alone?' She tried to hide the panic in her voice but she didn't manage it. It was very clear to her own ears, and to Cole's, judging by the sardonic twist of his lips.

'I'm not going to eat you,' he said drily. 'I thought the two of us could be adult enough to sit and have a civilised lunch together, but if you're too frightened...' He allowed his voice to trail off scornfully.

'Of course I'm not frightened.' She denied the accusation quickly and forcefully. There was no way she wanted Cole to think he intimidated her; that was the last straw to break her flagging self-esteem.

'Good, then we can sit and talk in a rational manner.' There was a brief gleam of satisfied amusement in his dark eyes.

Talk about what? Lauren wondered with a pang of nerves as he took her by the arm and led her in a none too gentle way towards the exit of the palace. And why did she feel as if she had just been very cleverly manoeuvred into not being able to refuse the daunting invitation?

Cole held up his hand and stopped a taxi. There was a few minutes' delay while he told the driver he wanted to go to River City and arranged what the fare would be. Then they climbed in and the driver took off at breakneck speed down the busy roads.

'So where are we going?' Lauren asked.

'I told you—lunch,' he said easily.

Lauren glanced out at the teeming traffic and people, her mind struggling to come up with some reason why they were going for lunch alone. Why hadn't Donna come along?

The taxi careered around a corner, sending her flying against Cole's shoulder, and he put out an arm to steady her.

'Sorry.' She pulled away abruptly, the contact making her nerves tingle.

'That's OK.' The attractive lips curved in a grin. 'Driving isn't for the timid out here, is it?'

'No, I suppose not.' Lauren kept her eyes away from him and on the fast-flowing traffic, the motorbikes carrying adults and children, the buses and lorries all weaving in and out without checking their speed. Her heart was thudding wildly, but it had nothing to do with the chaotic roads; it was entirely due to the man sitting next to her.

She didn't want to be alone with him; her nervous system felt as if it was on a knife-edge. When he had touched her a moment ago she had felt everything inside her burn with apprehension.

The taxi pulled up and the driver turned to them with a smile to tell them in halting English that they had reached their destination.

The heat of the street was a shock after the air-conditioned cool of the car. Cole put a casual arm at her back to guide her through the crowds and then they were walking into the tranquil coolness of a very ornate restaurant.

A waiter came up to them immediately and without too much fuss they were shown to the best table in the house and presented with a menu.

'The English is at the back,' Cole told her as he noticed her flicking through the pages of different languages. 'The Thai food is very good in here if you'd like to try some.'

Right at this moment Lauren didn't want anything to eat. She felt downright uncomfortable with this whole situation. Why were they out having lunch together? Where was Donna? Surely she couldn't be too pleased about her fiancé having dinner with his ex-girlfriend?

'Are you ready to order?' Cole asked her now as a waiter approached.

Lauren looked down at the various choices in front of her on the menu. She had been so distracted by her own thoughts that she hadn't even read them. But she nodded and just chose the first thing that caught her eye.

'I don't think you'll like that, Lauren,' Cole said calmly. 'I think it will be a little too spicy for your taste. The tiger prawns are good—why don't you try them?'

'OK, anything.' Lauren closed the menu with an impatient snap. She just wanted this ordeal to be over; it was pure torture sitting opposite him like this. It brought back memories that she had worked very hard at burying.

She listened as he ordered the wine. He knew her tastes exactly, both in food and in drink. But then you didn't live with someone for nearly a year without discovering his or her likes and dislikes. He knew that she didn't like anything too spicy. She knew that he liked his steak well done. It was most disconcerting sitting across the table from him trying to act like a total stranger.

He looked across at her and their eyes collided. He smiled. 'You looked as if you were a million miles away there. What were you thinking about?'

She shrugged slender shoulders. Naturally dark lashes veiled her blue eyes for a moment. She wasn't about to tell him what had just been running through her mind; it was verging too much on the personal. 'I was wondering where Donna is? Didn't she want to come along with us?'

'I have an idea she wasn't too pleased at being sent back to the hotel.' His lips twisted in an attractive grin for a moment before he said more seriously, 'I didn't want her to come along, I wanted it to be just the two of us.'

Puzzled blue eyes flew to his face.

'I'm sorry about this morning, Lauren,' he continued in a gravel-deep tone. 'I didn't mean to upset you—that's the last thing I want.'

Lauren's heart thudded painfully against her ribs. She didn't want Cole to start being kind; that would make everything harder. She wanted to keep angry with him, then maybe she could get through this without becoming emotional.

'Let's just forget it, Cole,' she murmured. Much to her relief, the waiter arrived with their wine at that moment so the subject was dropped.

They sat in silence while he uncorked it and poured it for Cole to taste.

'That's fine.' Cole indicated that the man could leave them and leaned over to pour Lauren's drink himself.

'To us,' he said as he lifted his crystal goblet over towards her.

She frowned. 'That toast is most inappropriate,' she told him in a frosty tone.

'Is it?' He shrugged lightly and took a sip from the sparkling wine before replacing the glass down next to him. 'I don't see why.'

'Well, I would think it's pretty obvious.' Her voice held an angry edge now. 'There is no *us*.'

'Really? Then how come we're sitting here having lunch together?' he asked with dry amusement. 'Don't tell me that it's a figment of my imagination? That we aren't really here, that it's two other people sitting sharing a bottle of wine and a meal?'

'Don't be facetious,' she snapped in a cool tone. 'You know exactly what I mean.'

'No, I don't.' He grinned at her. 'Why don't you tell me?'

She glared at him. He was baiting her, deliberately, enjoying the spark of anger he was creating. 'I don't need to spell it out, Cole. I think it's pretty clear even to someone as insensitive as you,' she said loftily.

One dark eyebrow rose. 'Do you think I'm insensitive?'

'I just said so, didn't I?' Lauren reached for her wine glass, irritated beyond measure by the conversation.

'Is this observation based on your experience with me in the past?' he asked drily. 'Or have I neglected to order your favourite aperitif?'

Lauren put her wine glass down with a thump on the linen tablecloth and glared at him with eyes that burned with anger.

'OK, OK.' He held up his hands in mock surrender. 'Let's call a truce on this, shall we? Otherwise I can see me ducking out of the way of flying crockery.' His mouth curved in that captivating grin of his. 'Why don't we just relax and enjoy lunch like two old friends? After all the time we've spent together in the past, we should at least be able to do that, surely?'

She shrugged, her anger fading to discomfort. 'As I said before, I think it's too late for us to be friends.'

'I don't believe that, Lauren,' he said softly. 'I know that the last part of our relationship wasn't exactly happy. But we did have good times.' His eyes held hers steadily. 'Didn't we?' he asked in a low tone.

She looked away from him and swallowed hard. She didn't want to be reminded of happy times. She didn't even want to admit to herself that there had been any, let alone admit it to him.

The silence stretched for a strained couple of minutes, then the waiter arrived with their starter. They both sat quietly while he served them. Then as soon as he left Cole returned to the subject.

'We did have some happy times, Lauren. I don't believe you don't remember them as such.'

'I'm here to do an article on you, Cole, not dig up the past.' She kept her voice crisply cool with a tremendous effort.

'Do you remember our first evening at the ranch in California?' he persisted tenaciously. 'How I wanted to take you out for a meal but you insisted on cooking dinner?'

She smiled. 'I burnt it horribly and you said it was the best thing you had ever tasted.' The recollection flew spontaneously to her lips.

'It was.' His dark eyes gleamed with a look that made her heart flip wildly. 'Especially the dessert,' he added with soft emphasis.

'Cole!' She looked away, her cheeks flaring with bright colour at the intimate memory of exactly what dessert had consisted of.

'We did have good times, Lauren, and I did care about you...more than you want to believe.'

But he was still about to marry another woman, Lauren thought, her mind swiftly rejecting the sentimental statement.

She put down her knife and fork, her food barely touched. 'Just where is this all leading, Cole?' she demanded briskly. 'I really don't see the point of rehashing things that are dead and gone.'

The dark eyes held hers for a moment before he shrugged. 'I guess I just wanted us to be at ease with each other. Even if it's just for old times' sake.'

Everything inside her screamed out against the suggestion. She didn't want to be at ease, especially for old times' sake, but it seemed churlish to say that. 'I don't know,' she murmured instead. 'It's all very well spouting about us just being friends but there are other people to consider now. People who might be hurt or misconstrue a friendship between us.'

He frowned. 'I suppose you're thinking about Jon?' he grated roughly. 'I'm not going to beat about the bush, Lauren; I just don't like the guy and I really don't give a damn what he thinks.'

Lauren had actually been thinking more of Donna, but she immediately flew to her colleague's defence. 'That's not fair, Cole. You hardly know Jon and he really is a nice guy.'

The waiter arrived to clear away their dishes. Lauren noticed that, like her, Cole had barely touched the delicious starter. The main course was placed before them. Lauren glanced down at the enormous prawns, usually one of her favourites, but somehow could generate no enthusiasm for the food.

'Jon has a good eye for a beautiful woman,' Cole grated scornfully. 'Not only has he been flirting with you this morning but he's been positively leering at Donna. I don't particularly think that makes for a nice guy.'

Lauren frowned. Was Cole so possessive over Donna that he was jealous about the way another man looked at her? 'I think you're being unnecessarily harsh on him. I'm sure he has looked at Donna and thought her attractive. He would hardly be a red-blooded male if the thought hadn't crossed his mind. But I don't for one moment think he's been leering at her.'

Cole shrugged. 'If you say so.'

There was silence for a moment while they both concentrated on their meals. Lauren's thoughts were far away. Cole must be very much in love with Donna to worry about the way other men looked at her. It surprised her that he should be so jealous. Cole was so supremely confident in all things. Surely he realised that Donna was so completely infatuated with him that she would never stray?

'What do you really think of Richards?' Cole asked suddenly now.

'I've told you. He's a genuine kind of man. Good at his job, good fun. I like him. I don't think you need worry about him.'

'Who said I was worried about him?' Cole frowned. 'I said I didn't like him, but I have no reason to worry over him.' He put down his cutlery and leaned across to refill her glass. 'Have you been working with him long?'

She nodded. 'Well, since I returned after...' Her voice trailed away awkwardly. She had been about to say after their relationship had ended, but that hardly seemed an appropriate thing to mention. She wanted so much to forget that there had been anything between them.

'After we split up.' He finished her sentence drily. 'It's all right, Lauren, I do know that we split up,' he continued in a sarcastic vein. 'You're not letting out a state secret.' He picked up his own glass and watched the different expressions flicker over her delicate features.

She was irritated by his manner, but at the same time she was hurt by how easily he was able to talk about the past, as if all it had been was a brief, meaningless affair.

'So you've been working closely with Richards ever since you went back to work for the paper?' he went on now.

'I suppose so,' she replied absently.

'Are you enjoying it as much as you thought you would?'

'What?' She glanced over at him, puzzled.

'Being back at work—are you enjoying it?' he repeated, a note of impatience in the smooth tone.

'Yes. I love it,' she answered him truthfully. She did enjoy her work. It kept her busy, it kept her mind off the past. Or rather, it used to keep her mind off the past. 'Look, Cole, instead of making polite small talk like this, how about talking about the article I've come to write?' Suddenly she was impatient herself. This was utterly ridiculous. They shouldn't be sitting here like this. It was getting her nowhere.

'What do you want to know?' He signalled to the waiter that they had finished their meal.

'Well, for a start, what date is set for your wedding...where exactly it will take place?'

He smiled at that, but it was a smile singularly lacking in any real amusement. 'You'll have to be patient, Lauren,' he said in a low tone. 'You'll have to practise patience just as I'm doing.'

Her blue eyes met his, a puzzled light in their clear depths. 'What do you mean by that?'

'I mean, my dear Lauren, that as usual work is going to have to take a front seat. But I hope that won't be the case for much longer.' He glanced at his watch. 'And unfortunately it is time that we were moving. I told the crew two o'clock, and it's nearly that now.'

Annoyance flared at his complete avoidance of her questions. 'Well, can you give me any idea of when you will be able to answer my questions?' she asked crisply.

'Not at the moment...no.' He paid the waiter and rose to his feet. 'If you're ready?'

She got up, feeling very much like a small child being told what to do, not a professional journalist here to do a job.

Cole led the way out of the restaurant. 'I really wanted to take you up to the shopping complex at River City,' he said as they got outside. 'I wanted to ask your opinion on some new furniture I'm thinking of buying for the ranch.'

'New furniture?' she echoed him hollowly, suddenly realising why he had invited her out to lunch without Donna. He wanted her to help him choose a gift for their home together!

'I thought some new bedroom furniture would be a good idea——'

'I'm really not interested, Cole,' she cut across him sharply, anger boiling up inside her at such insensitivity. 'I don't want to know about your personal plans for your home. All I want to know is when your wedding will take place, so that I can arrange my story and get on the first available flight home.'

His lips tightened in a firm line. 'Why the big hurry to get home?'

'Jon and I have deadlines to meet, other assignments waiting,' she told him briskly. 'We can't afford to waste too much time out here.'

'Quite the cosy little team, aren't you?' His voice held a low, jeering note now.

'I suppose we are.' She wanted to say 'almost as cosy as you and Donna' but she held her tongue; this situation wasn't going to be helped by them both sniping at each other.

'Well, we'll go straight back, then. I wouldn't want to detain you.' Cole stepped out on to the street and hailed a taxi. 'We should be wrapping things up this afternoon,' he told her grimly, as he held the door of the car for her to get in. 'I want to be on a plane to Phuket by tomorrow morning. Then you will get your story. Happy?'

'Perfectly,' she snapped primly, and sat staring straight ahead as he got in the taxi beside her.

But the truth of the matter was that happiness had never seemed so far away, Lauren thought as they travelled back in complete silence. Obviously Cole's wedding was to take place at Phuket, and right at this moment she didn't think she could face it.

CHAPTER FOUR

THEY left Bangkok early the next morning. Five long black limousines took them to the airport and from there they split up, the camera crew, Jon and some of the group taking a scheduled Thai Airways flight to Phuket. The rest of them travelled with Cole on his private plane.

An hour later Lauren was glancing out of the window down at clear turquoise waters, lush green hills and long stretches of white sand.

'I can't wait to laze on one of those beaches,' Donna murmured as she turned her attention away from the magazine she had been reading throughout the flight.

'Well, it won't be long now, sweetheart.' Cole looked back at her from the controls of the plane and grinned. 'I'd say one more day like we had yesterday and we'll be finished work.'

'Wonderful!' She leaned back into her seat and closed the magazine. She looked incredibly sexy in a very short white miniskirt and an apple-green off-the-shoulder top.

Lauren, sitting across the aisle from her, felt almost dowdy in her cool yellow sundress.

'The first thing I'm going to do when we get into the hotel is book an appointment at the beauty salon,' Donna continued. 'Perhaps you should do the same, Lauren,' she added with an archly sweet smile across at her.

'What Lauren does is up to her, but the first thing that you are going to do is change into that skimpy bikini and let the camera crew get some shots of you down on the beach,' Cole corrected her gently.

She shook long glossy hair impatiently. 'The guys are right about you, Cole. You really are a slave-driver.'

'The sooner we get started, the sooner we get finished,' he replied easily. 'Now, better fasten your seatbelts: I'm about to put this baby down.'

As Donna moved to comply, her magazine slid off her knee and landed in the aisle. Glancing down, Lauren noticed that it was an American fashion book with a special feature on bridal style. She bent to retrieve it for the other girl.

'Looking for a special dress?' she asked conversationally.

'I bought some silk in Bangkok and I'm going to have it made up to a design I like in here.' Donna flicked over the glossy pages and handed her the picture of the dress.

'It's beautiful.' Lauren felt strangely numb as she looked down at the white dress. It wasn't a traditional style for a wedding dress. The skirt was full but short, showing the model's long, slim legs. The bodice was fitted in to the tiny waist and patterned with mother-of-pearl. It was a very modern style, and she could just see Donna in it.

'Yes, it is,' Donna agreed enthusiastically. 'I can't wait to have it made up. There is a designer boutique at the hotel we'll be staying at. I'm going to ask if they'll do it for me.'

'You should have something made up for yourself, Lauren,' Cole put in now. 'We're having a party tomorrow night to celebrate the end of work.'

Lauren didn't particularly feel like celebrating anything, but she forbore to comment.

The plane banked and Cole brought it down smoothly on to the runway of Phuket Airport.

It was about an hour's drive out to their beach resort. The drive was a pleasant one through tropically lush countryside of rice fields, coconut and rubber plantations. Donna sat up front next to Cole, who was driving, and they talked about the remaining work that had to be done on the video.

'I thought we'd take a few shots of you coming out of the water, your hair slicked back off your face, your bikini wet as if you'd just finished an energetic swim,' Cole was saying easily.

'You mean a sexy shot, those lovely lips pouting, the curvaceous, tanned body gleaming with water and very little else,' Jed put in with a grin.

'Something like that,' Cole agreed with a laugh. 'Donna is going to be the hottest item on the music scene after I've finished with her.'

'Are you thinking of going it alone in the music business, Donna?' Lauren asked her curiously.

'Well, I'm going to do a solo album, but I won't be alone exactly. I'll have Cole to help and guide me.' One slender hand moved to his shoulders and rested there in a possessive gesture. 'Won't I, darling?'

'Yes, I think we are going to be stuck with each other for a while,' he agreed with dry humour.

'Don't say it like that.' She looked up at him, her green eyes wide and appealing. 'You make it sound as if you're not looking forward to us being together. I know I've been a bit trying recently, but I'll make it up to you.' Red-tipped fingers trailed teasingly up through his dark hair. 'Promise,' she murmured huskily.

He grinned. 'Just look at the camera like that when we start filming this afternoon and I'll forgive you anything.'

Lauren turned her eyes out towards the passing countryside and tried to switch her ears and her mind off the flirtatious repartee.

Cole turned the car into an impressive entrance. The wrought-iron gates were flanked by trailing deep pink bougainvillaea, that partially covered the sign proclaiming they were at 'The Hideaway'. Two security guards came forward and Cole wound down the electric windows of the car to speak to them. 'Cole Adams,' he said in a brisk tone.

A few seconds later, after his name had been carefully checked off on their list, the gates swung open and they were driving up a long driveway flanked by tall palm trees that threw cool dark shade over the lush, colourful gardens.

The hotel was a long, low white building covered in creeping vines and flowers. Cole pulled up outside the front entrance and a doorman came down the few steps from the long glass doors to open the car doors for them.

The air held the sweet, fresh fragrance of flowers and Lauren breathed deeply as they got out of the car. 'This is beautiful!'

'True paradise,' Cole agreed with a grin.

'Well, it is one of *the* hotels of the region,' Donna said nonchalantly. 'A lot of celebrities stay here because it's a private retreat. They know that once they get here they won't be bothered by the gutter Press. No photographers can breach security and no tacky little reporters——' Donna broke off and clamped a hand to her mouth. 'That was rather tactless of me, wasn't it? Sorry, Lauren.'

Lauren shook her head, a wry smile curving her lips. 'That's all right, Donna. I've never thought of myself as a tacky little reporter. No offence taken,' she said lightly. Yet at the back of her mind she knew somehow that the remark had been intentionally offensive. That was Donna's way; she had made many a barbed remark in the past. 'By the sound of it I'm lucky to have been allowed to stay.'

'Actually I have had to vouch for you,' Cole grinned. 'The guests are put through a kind of screening process. It's just to make sure no one is bothered by the media.

A lot of the people who stay here are very newsworthy and the guy who owns the hotel goes to a lot of trouble to make sure this is one place where they don't have to worry about a photographer springing out when they've just put on a bikini or kissed someone they shouldn't. It's owned by Drew Sheldon, the same man who owns the Bangkok Sheldon.' They walked up the steps and through the front doors into a world of total luxury and elegance.

The hotel was smaller and more intimate than the one they had stayed in in Bangkok. The foyer was furnished with a style that could only belong to the Far East, where charm and beauty were achieved with a great simplicity. A jade vase filled with white orchids was reflected on the highly polished table, deep settees and chairs had hand-painted rich motifs of exotic birds against the soft white silk covers.

The carpets were the same dazzling shade of turquoise as the Andaman Sea that you could see through the long sliding glass doors that led out to a terrace of flowers.

A young Thai girl welcomed them with a lovely smile at the reception desk. 'Hello, Mr Adams. We are so pleased to have you stay with us again.'

As Cole signed the register, two bellboys arrived to show them to their rooms.

'Has the rest of my party arrived yet?' Cole asked the receptionist.

'No, not yet, Mr Adams.'

Donna grinned. 'No camera crew—great; that means I can go and have a relaxing session in the beauty salon.'

'Don't go disappearing on me,' Cole told her warily. 'They won't be long, and I want to start work immediately once they get here.'

'I've got time for a facial, surely?' Donna enquired sulkily. 'The crew will want to have lunch before they start work, and I need to relax a little, Cole; I want to look my best for our big day.'

'You'll look beautiful,' Cole assured her lazily. 'You always do. But go on; you can have one hour.'

'Thanks, darling.' She reached up and kissed his cheek. 'See you later, then.'

He watched her go with a grin on his attractive features. 'I don't know why Donna is so nervous about all this. She's going to look sensational.' Turning, he caught Lauren's eye. 'How about having lunch with me out on the terrace?' he invited casually.

'No, thanks, I'm going to do some work,' she replied coolly. She couldn't go through that ordeal again. Being alone with Cole was definitely to be avoided for her peace of mind.

'Oh?' One dark eyebrow lifted sardonically. 'But I am your work, am I not?'

'If you're inviting me to interview you, then——'

'How can you interview me without your right-hand man?' he interrupted her, his voice faintly jeering. 'I didn't think you as much as sneezed these days without having Jon by your side to capture the moment, and as he has been detained I thought we would relax for a little while. Of course, I was forgetting that you didn't do anything that decadent these days.'

'I relax when my work is finished,' she told him angrily.

'There was a time when I could distract you from work without too much difficulty,' he said in a voice that was disturbingly low and husky. 'I think the *Global Record* newspaper has sent me the wrong Lauren Martin.'

'On the contrary, they've sent the right one... this time.' Her voice was carefully modulated. 'I have my priorities in good order these days, Cole, and I won't be side-tracked or sweet-talked or distracted in any way from the job I've come to do.'

Dark eyes swept over her face in a deeply contemplative way. 'We'll see,' he drawled huskily. 'We'll see.'

Lauren turned away from him, a frown marring her smooth complexion. If he had been hoping to amuse himself with her for an hour or two while he waited for Donna, he could think again. Heavens, that man had some arrogant nerve! The way he had so calmly expected her to help him choose furniture for him and Donna yesterday still stung her deeply. Did he imagine that his attraction was so great that she could forget how much he had hurt her in the past? That they could just calmly act like old friends and forget everything that had happened? How could she ever have fallen for such a conceited, cold-hearted man? she wondered angrily as she followed the bellboy towards her room.

The room was exceptionally beautiful: a huge double bed covered with rich blue silk covers, white carpets, heavy silk curtains at the long glass doors that led out on to a secluded garden with its own winding path down to where palm trees fringed an empty white beach.

For a while Lauren stood and looked out. A gentle breeze was making the waves roll in and break against the shore in lacy white foam. It was the type of scene that you looked at on the idyllic posters of a travel agent's wall and wished you could be there. Would Cole and Donna be married under the palm trees down there? Or out on the terrace of flowers that she had glimpsed as they entered the hotel?

She turned away from the view with a sigh. Well, all she could say was that Donna was welcome to him. He was a man totally obsessed with his work; a life with him would not be to her taste. She wondered what would happen if Donna ever decided she wanted to start a family.

The question disturbed her intensely and she pushed it away as she started to unpack her case. What did she care what would happen? She was here to work; she'd get her story and get on the first available plane back to England and forget about them.

She took a white cotton T-shirt and a red skirt from among her clothes and went into the bathroom to shower and change.

When she came out she decided to jot down a few notes on the article she was to write. Better to make a start, put down a few of the questions she would ask Cole and get things clear in her mind. She opened up her briefcase and sat down at the bureau, which was placed strategically by the glass doors so that you could look out over the lawns.

She wrote a couple of lines. 'Twenty-three-year-old Donna Wade is set to have all her dreams come true: a breakthrough into the big time for her career in music, and marriage to one of today's most eligible bachelors.' Then she stared down at the stark words on the white page.

Strange how memories could come back to haunt you at the most inappropriate moments. She didn't want to think about the past; she wanted to do this job with a professional, detached attitude. Yet she couldn't seem to help herself thinking back.

Back then, giving up her job to tour with Cole had seemed like a logical move. Nothing else had mattered to Lauren except their being together. And at first it had all been idyllic.

There had been a month in California staying at his ranch. Then he had started his world tour and they had travelled extensively. Everywhere they went, Cole had played to packed auditoriums, adoring fans had mobbed him, and the media had followed his every step.

She had written a few articles about his tour and they had been snapped up. Everyone wanted to know the inside story, the real Cole Adams. Cole had called her his PR girl and in a way it had been a job; it had certainly occupied most of her spare time. It was only when they got towards the end of the tour in Australia that things had started to go wrong.

Lauren had stopped writing for a while; she was feeling tired, the heat was making her feel ill and suddenly living out of a suitcase didn't seem as exciting as it had once been. When her time wasn't fully occupied with her own work she realised how little time Cole was spending with her. And suddenly she noticed how much time he spent with Donna.

She wasn't the jealous type, and she told herself that she was being fanciful. But she couldn't help noticing how Cole enthused over Donna's voice, her looks, her professionalism. Then she noticed how Donna looked at him, and it struck her out of nowhere that the other woman was in love with Cole.

The tour ended and they went back to the ranch in California so that Cole could start work on a new album. Lauren thought that when they got back to a real home they would have more time together. But it was almost worse than it was before. Cole spent all his days at the recording studio with the group; sometimes he didn't come home until the early hours of the morning. Lauren felt isolated; she had no real part of Cole's life, whereas Donna was very much a part of it.

Then she discovered that she was pregnant, and everything just seemed to fall apart after that. The thought of having Cole's baby thrilled her to her very core. Deep down she thought that Cole would be pleased too, but she wasn't sure. She waited patiently for a few weeks, trying to find the right time to tell him. But the right time never seemed to come. He left in the early hours of the morning, and when he returned it was late and he was tired.

On the one and only day off he had had in months he invited Donna to join them at the ranch for the day and the two of them spent the time cooped up in the private recording studio he had had built on.

When Donna finally left it was nearly midnight. Lauren, waiting in the bedroom for Cole to come up, was feeling tired and more than a little tearful.

'You're still up!' He looked surprised to see her sitting up in bed. 'I'm totally shattered.' He went through to the bathroom to switch on the shower, and when he returned he was unbuttoning his shirt. 'Donna is really something else. Her voice just seems to get better and better. I think she will be a big star in her own right one day.'

'Really?' Lauren tried to sound interested. 'Must be all the extra time you're spending with her—some of your genius must be rubbing off.' There was an edge to her tone but Cole didn't seem to notice.

'I think I might give her a solo spot on my next album.' He put his shirt down on the chair and sat down to take off his shoes. His skin was smooth and tanned; his muscles gleamed bronze in the lamplight. He looked so attractive that Lauren could feel a lump coming into her throat.

'Cole, we need to talk.' She blurted the words out suddenly.

'Oh?' His voice sounded wary; he stopped what he was doing and glanced up at her. 'This isn't going to be heavy, is it, Lauren?'

'Strange how you've got so much time to spare for Donna and none at all for me,' she said quietly.

'Now you are being silly.' He raked a hand impatiently through thick dark hair. 'I work with Donna. What's all this about, Lauren?'

She shrugged, suddenly at a loss for words now that she had his complete attention. 'I don't know... I feel... left out or something.' She stopped and swallowed hard. 'I know this sounds strange, but I just feel as if we are both going in different directions.'

'I see.' His voice was gravel-deep. 'And what sort of direction do you want to be taking?'

She hesitated. 'I don't know... I just know that I want something... I want to feel secure. When I was at the newspaper I at least felt as if I belonged; here I just feel out of place.'

'You want to start work again?' He leaned back against the chair, his dark eyes raking her pale features.

'I want... I want to know where we're going, I want something that's more secure. A home, family...'

'If you are looking for a nine-to-five man then you've got the wrong guy, Lauren,' he answered steadily. 'As for a family... I'm not ready for that kind of commitment, and I'm not going to bring a child into this world unless I can offer it a very secure home life.'

Lauren felt as if someone had just punched her. 'I see...' There was a long silence and then as he got to his feet she just had to say something. 'You mean, if I told you I was pregnant you would be less than pleased?'

She watched the different expressions crossing his face, and of all of them anger was predominant. 'This isn't something to joke about,' he grated harshly.

She held his gaze and forced herself to continue. 'So really what you're saying is that I'm just a casual affair and you have no interest in taking our relationship further.'

He turned away from her. She had never before realised how powerfully disapproving a back could be. She wanted to go to him, to put her arms around him. She wanted him to hold her, to reassure her.

'I'm too tired for this nonsense, Lauren,' he told her in an acid tone. 'And quite frankly I'm astounded that you could try to pull a stunt like this.'

She frowned, not following him at all. 'I don't understand, Cole—what do you mean by——?'

'I mean that I know exactly what you are doing and I'm not going to stand for it,' he rasped furiously. 'I won't be bulldozed into making a commitment that I'm not ready to make.'

She flinched, her blood literally running cold. 'You think I'm a scheming woman out to trap you?' There was bitter amusement in the low, husky tone.

'I think that it's late and I'm exhausted and quite frankly the last thing I need right now is a conversation about marriage and children,' he said bluntly, then without another glance in her direction he moved through into the bathroom, closing the door behind him with a quiet click.

She lay where she was for a long time, listening to the sound of his shower, her body in a state of numb shock. Then she picked up her things and moved to the room next door.

Even as she lay alone in the darkness of that room she thought that maybe Cole would come to her. She had never felt so frightened and so alone, and she couldn't accept the fact that Cole didn't love her.

I'm not ready for that kind of commitment. She could hear those words again as clearly as if she were back in that bedroom in California. Obviously that sentiment had changed now that he was sure he had the right woman. Would his thoughts about having children have changed as well? Would she have to ask him if he and Donna wanted a family when she interviewed him?

She pushed herself away from the desk and paced restlessly around the room. Then on impulse she opened the glass doors out into the garden and stepped into the sunshine. She couldn't do any more writing; she couldn't even think straight.

She could hear the tide thundering against the shore, and somewhere a bird was calling. A sudden loud splash made her turn. A little to her left a large swimming-pool glittered in the bright sunlight. A man was swimming with sure, powerful strokes through the brilliant blue of the water. As she watched he hauled himself out at the far side. Bronzed muscles flexed as he reached for a towel and used it to rub the thick dark head of hair. She didn't need to look twice to know it was Cole. She knew that lithe, superbly fit body so well. The broad shoulders were powerfully awesome, and for a moment she found herself remembering how good it had felt to be held against that strong chest.

'Seen enough?' he enquired with lazy humour as he draped the towel around those shoulders and his eyes locked with hers.

Silky blonde hair swung as she moved away from him and down towards the beach. She wasn't going to justify that teasing, infuriating question with a reply. She had only just glanced at him; she wasn't interested enough to stare.

'Running away?' He caught up with her easily as she stopped to take her sandals off once she reached the soft white sand.

'Why should I be running away?' She swung around to face him and then wished she hadn't as she found herself uncomfortably close, with her eyes on a level with that broad chest. It glistened with silver droplets of water in the sunlight. She took a hasty step back from him.

The firm mouth slanted in a grin. 'You look nervous. What's the matter, sweetheart?'

'Nothing, and don't call me that.' Her voice sounded brittle.

'Why not?' he asked, and his tone dropped to a husky, intimate note. 'After all, that is what you used to be—my sweetheart.'

'"Used" being the operative word,' she murmured bitterly. 'And I was never your sweetheart. Your "concubine" would probably be a more apt description; there was nothing very sweet about that.'

'No?' One dark eyebrow rose and the way his eyes burnt down on her pale skin made her heart thud crazily. 'I can think of one or two very sweet moments.'

He moved closer and reached one hand out to rest it on her shoulder. The simple touch was like a brand of fire through the thin cotton of her T-shirt. 'Can't you remember any of them, Laurie?' he asked in a low tone.

She shook her head. She didn't want to remember any sweet moments; she wanted to remember cold words, lonely nights.

'I've been trying to make a start on the article I've to write.' She forced herself to talk business, her tone brisk. 'I've jotted down a few questions, the usual kind of thing. When do you think we can sit down to discuss it all?'

He shrugged his shoulders, then without warning his hand moved gently to her face and trailed softly through her hair. Dark eyes moved over her pale skin and lingered on her lips. 'How about dinner tonight?'

Her heart pounded heavily at the invitation. 'You mean the four of us, I take it?'

He shook his head. 'No, I mean the two of us,' he replied easily.

She frowned and shook her head. 'Cole, why are you making things so difficult? I need Jon with me when I interview you——'

'Why?' he cut across her crisply. 'You managed perfectly well when you came to interview me on my own once before.' His mouth curved in a very attractive grin. 'Why do you suddenly need Jon along to hold your hand?'

And look what had happened that time! Lauren remembered with mounting panic. 'Because...because I just do,' she murmured helplessly.

'Because you're afraid of being alone with me,' he said in a self-assured tone. 'Because you still feel attracted to me.'

For a moment Lauren stared at him, absolutely horrified by the words, her face slowly turning a bright crimson-red. 'Of all the conceited...' She trailed off, for a moment at a complete loss for words before blazing angrily, 'I know how you like to believe every woman is in love with you, but I'm afraid you'll have to strike me off your fan-mail list.' Her voice dripped scorn. 'I told you in London that I no longer felt anything for you, Cole. I meant it then and I certainly mean it now.'

He shook his head and there was a hard glitter in his dark eyes now. It was obvious that he didn't like to be reminded of that episode; his ego couldn't take the fact that she had been for even one brief moment impervious to him. 'You were upset back then, Lauren; you weren't thinking clearly.'

'On the contrary, my thoughts were crystal-clear. I had come to my senses at last. I would have thought that was very plain—even to someone as conceited as you. You kissed me and there was absolutely nothing there— no feeling at all. I think that must have told you much plainer than any words how I felt about you.'

'It told me that you were upset, that you needed time to put things into perspective,' he told her grimly.

'I'd already had plenty of time to put things into perspective,' she retorted furiously. 'Five long weeks, to be exact, before you bothered to come and see me.'

'It was your decision to leave California and go back to London,' he grated harshly. 'I didn't ask you to leave.'

Lauren pursed her lips angrily. He hadn't exactly left her with any choice other than to leave him. The fact that he liked to conveniently forget that was typical of the man. He didn't want to accept any guilt, any responsibility for anything. 'No, you didn't ask me to leave, Cole, you just called me a liar and a devious, underhanded woman who was out to trap you—but you're right; you didn't ask me to leave.' Her voice trembled alarmingly as she recalled those terrible accusations. They had hurt so much... surprisingly, they still did.

'Lauren, I——'

'No, Cole, I don't want to talk about this, for one minute more,' she cut across him, her eyes blazing a bright vivid blue. How on earth had they got on to such a personal level with this conversation? All she wanted was to remain businesslike, and he kept breaking her cool with the utmost ease.

'I think you've conveniently forgotten just how badly our... our affair ended, otherwise you would never be so stupid as to try your usual flirtatious repartee out on me,' she said now, raking an unsteady hand through her hair.

He shook his head. 'I haven't forgotten anything, Lauren. On the contrary, I remember everything about you very clearly.' His voice was a soft, husky drawl. 'I especially remember how good things were between us once. I think it's you who has forgotten. You've forgotten how you used to melt in my arms, how you used to respond to my kisses.' His fingers moved to softly trace the outline of her lips.

Lauren stared at him, her heart pounding with a mixture of nerves and anger. She never failed to be amazed by his arrogance. Even though he was engaged to Donna, he still liked to think that if he wanted her he could have her as he could have any other woman. His conceited attitude just made her blood boil.

His head moved closer and she stiffened.

'I hope you're not going to kiss me, Cole.' Her voice was quite crisp, quite controlled. 'Because I would hate to have to slap your face.'

One eyebrow lifted and a glimmer of amusement returned to the dark eyes now. 'Somehow I gain the impression from you that you would be glad of any excuse to slap my face.' His lips twisted in an arrogantly handsome grin. 'Maybe I should kiss you, then you can slap me and we will have cleared the air,' he murmured drolly.

She brushed his hand away angrily. 'You really are one arrogant son-of-a——'

She never got to finish the sentence, because one moment she was blazing out the words in fury and the next his lips were over hers.

It wasn't a passionate kiss; it was too brief, too controlled for that. He was playing a game of some sort with her, testing out her response. He was probably so used to women throwing themselves at him that he just wanted to prove to her that she was no different.

Much to her disgust, she did start to respond: her lips softened instinctively beneath his, her hand rested for a short moment against the broad bare chest. Only because he had caught her by surprise, she assured herself grimly—that was the only reason her lips had clung for that instant.

'How dare you?' She choked the words out furiously, like a person in the midst of drowning coming up for air. 'How dare you do that?'

'Don't get carried away, Lauren,' he said. 'It wasn't that big a deal.'

'Not that big a deal?' she repeated, like some halfwit too shocked to do anything else.

A half-smile tugged at his lips. 'I just wanted to show you that there really is nothing to be afraid of.'

She shook her head. If that kiss had shown her anything, it was that there was definitely something to be afraid of. 'I find your attitude and your behaviour totally reprehensible.' Her eyes blazed over-bright and she was trembling all over; even her voice was shaking.

'You sound like some prim and proper old maid,' he muttered drily. 'It was just a kiss—forget it.'

Her hands clenched into tight fists at her side. She had forgotten how totally infuriating Cole could be; his arrogant manner, his laid-back attitude made her blood race like hot lava through her veins. 'Have you forgotten that I'm here to interview you about your forthcoming marriage?' she enquired furiously.

'No, Lauren, I have not.' He shrugged broad shoulders. Then he grinned. 'Would you like me to forget about it for a few hours?'

She took a deep, steadying breath. He was laughing at her—he actually had the gall to poke fun at her. 'What I would like, Cole, is to escape from here and never set eyes on you again. Ever,' she reiterated strongly.

He didn't seem bothered in the slightest, his lips twisting with lazy amusement. 'You sound as if you are doing a prison sentence, not staying at a luxury hotel in one of the world's most beautiful locations.'

'Even paradise would seem like hell if you were around,' she grated harshly.

'Really?' One finger tipped her chin up so that her blue eyes were forced to clash with his. 'You know what they say about people who protest too often and too intensely about something, don't you, Lauren?'

She moved away from him impatiently. 'I don't know what you're talking about.'

'No?' he drawled mockingly. 'Well, let me spell it out for you. They say it's a sign that your heart is still strongly involved.'

Her lips twisted scornfully. 'I hate so much to disillusion you, but my feelings for you are such that I can't think of one good word to write about you. You're a compulsive womaniser, an outrageous flirt——'

'I'm confident that you will do a good job. You managed to find complimentary things to write about me once before.' His tone was lazily amused.

'Cole, are you down here?' Donna's voice was calling from the direction of the pool, but Cole made no attempt to distance himself from Lauren.

'By the way,' he added in an undertone, and leaned even closer, 'you forgot to slap me.'

'There you are.' Donna appeared down beside them. Her green eyes narrowed as she noticed how close they were standing to each other.

Cole took his time stepping back from Lauren, but his voice was gently indulgent as he turned to the other woman. 'Yes, what is it, Donna?'

'The crew are here.' She stood with long legs slightly apart, bare feet burying into the soft white sand. She looked like a South Seas maiden, dark glossy hair lifted back from her delicate features by the soft sea breeze.

'OK, I'll be there in a moment.' Cole's voice was dismissive, but Donna didn't seem to notice.

'There seems to be some problem at the gate—security isn't letting them past,' she said briskly. 'The owner of the hotel is up there trying to sort it out, but I think you——'

'Drew's here?' She had his attention now.

'Out on the terrace with his wife,' she confirmed with a nod.

'Well, this is a surprise!' Cole grinned. 'OK, I'd better go and see what's going on.' He turned to Lauren. 'Coming?'

She shook her head. Her heart was still hammering like crazy. All she wanted right at this moment was to be left alone.

That, however, was not so easy to achieve because as Cole strode away back to the hotel Donna fell into step beside her as she turned to walk along the shore.

'You don't mind if I join you, do you, Lauren?' she enquired silkily.

Lauren minded a great deal, but to say so would have been unnecessarily rude. So she just shook her head.

The two girls walked in silence for a while. The beach was deserted, the creamy white sand curved in a crescent shape along the palm-lined shore. Out in the bay a small island was a colourful orb of green between the blue of the sky and the turquoise of the sea.

Lauren's mind wasn't on the scenery—it was still reeling in outrage from Cole's atrocious behaviour. He always had enjoyed baiting her, she remembered wryly. There was something about Cole that demanded a fiery, passionate response, but in the past the explosions when they had come had always ended in his arms. There had been times when she had suspected him of deliberately goading her in that direction.

'It's so beautiful here, isn't it?' Donna broke into the silence and her thoughts.

'Yes.' Lauren's answer was clipped. She was in no mood for small talk. Was Donna's relationship with Cole as tempestuous as theirs had been? she found herself wondering. The answer to that would have to be yes, for Cole was a very passionate man. There was no way he would think of marrying a woman who didn't match that side of his nature.

'Very romantic,' Donna went on, unperturbed by the stilted reply. 'Cole and I had a break here once before. I thought it was magical.'

Lauren glanced at her in surprise.

'Oh, it was before you and he were involved,' Donna informed her quickly.

'I see.' Lauren's voice sounded more than a little strained. Cole had not told her that he had been romantically involved with Donna before her, and somehow the fact that he hadn't really hurt. Desperately she tried to take the edge out of her voice; she wanted to sound unconcerned—after all, it was nothing to her what Cole did either before or after their relationship. 'It must be nice for you to return for such a...a momentous occasion,' she said lamely.

'Yes...perfect.' Donna sighed. 'I'm so lucky. I can hardly believe this is all happening. Cole has to be the most wonderful man in the world.'

Lauren's lips twisted wryly. She was sorely tempted to make some sarcastic reply, but to do so would sound as if she was jealous or something, and she certainly wasn't.

'Oh, I'm so sorry, Lauren, it was thoughtless of me to go on like that.' Donna shook her head. 'I can be so tactless at times; I hope I haven't upset you?'

'No, why should I be upset?' Lauren murmured calmly.

'Well...I was almost forgetting that you and Cole had a brief affair.' Donna smiled sympathetically at her, but the green eyes were cold. 'It must be hard for you, seeing him and knowing that it's all over between you, that he doesn't care about you.'

'It's not hard at all,' Lauren answered levelly. She felt like adding the words 'sorry to disappoint you', but she bit her lip and refrained. The girl was starting to grate on already raw nerves.

'I am glad. Cole said that you would be all right, that you were the right person to come and do the article about us. I must admit I had reservations. But as usual he was right. He said that what you'd had together was no more than a casual fling, that neither of you had ever been serious.'

The sea swirled in and caught their feet. The water felt warm against Lauren's chilled skin. Strange how she should suddenly feel so cold on such a hot day. It wasn't as if she cared what Cole had said. She didn't give one damn. This feeling of hurt was just her pride, that was all. She wished the woman would shut up; all her insides were screaming out at her to stop, to go away and leave her alone.

'I don't think I fully believed that at first,' Donna continued, seemingly oblivious to Lauren's silence. 'I couldn't believe that any woman could make love with Cole and not get serious.' She gave a small laugh. 'Well, we both know that men are capable of such things, and Cole is very red-blooded, if you know what I mean. But you——'

'What Cole and I felt about each other in the past is really none of your business, Donna,' Lauren interrupted suddenly, unable to listen to any more. She turned and looked directly at the other girl and anger was clearly evident in her stance, in the heat of her blue eyes.

Before she could say any more, Donna quickly apologised. 'I didn't mean to upset you, Lauren; honestly I didn't. I guess that having you around here is making me nervous.'

'Nervous?' Lauren shook her head. 'For a woman who is contemplating marriage, you don't seem to be very sure of your future husband.'

For a moment there was silence, and uncertainty was clear in the green eyes. 'What do you mean?' she asked with a frown.

'I mean that if you feel that you can't trust Cole then how can you possibly think about marrying him?'

'I'm not just thinking about marriage, I *am* going to marry him,' Donna asserted, her lips tightening. 'He's always been in love with me, you know, even before he met you. He just didn't realise it, not until he started to get bored with you. Then it hit him out of nowhere.'

'This is such a romantic tale, I just wish I'd brought my recorder,' Lauren said drily, then promptly wished she had said nothing. If she wanted to keep her dignity in all this she would have to make a determined effort not to sound bitter. 'So tell me, Donna, where and when did Cole propose to you?' She might as well get some information for her article while they were having this conversation, she decided firmly.

The look Donna slid over to her was venomous to say the least. 'He proposed soon after you moved out,' she said silkily. 'While we were in bed.' Her dark lashes lowered over the glittering green eyes. 'I do hope this is off the record, Lauren,' she added uncertainly. 'Cole would be furious if he knew I'd told you that.'

Not as furious as she felt right at this moment, Lauren thought wildly. It wasn't that she was jealous—what Cole did when she moved out had nothing to do with her at all.

'I didn't say yes at first,' Donna went on briskly. 'Well, I knew he still felt guilty about you. He had to go after you and find out if you were all right. He said he was afraid he'd broken your heart.'

'Oh, my heart is made of tougher stuff than that,' Lauren answered airily. 'And it was my decision not to go back to California. He did ask me.' She didn't know why she felt the need to say that. Inside her blood was thundering in angry waves through her body.

'Yes, he said he felt he had to ask you,' Donna murmured in an undertone. 'I think he felt sorry for you.'

Pain and pride flared in quick fury right the way through her. How dared Cole discuss her so blatantly with this woman? Just who did he think he was? In her mind's eye she could imagine them whispering about her. 'Poor Lauren, heartbroken Lauren.' The thought of their sympathy made her sick to her very stomach.

Donna swung to face her and there was a gleam of triumph in her beautiful eyes now. 'So you see, I do trust Cole.' She blurted the words out like a child pushing her point home. 'We love each other very much. And another little bit of information that you might not know: this is Cole's last album. He's giving up his career in music because he wants to settle down and spend more time with me. That's more than he was prepared to do for you, wasn't it, Lauren? He wouldn't even have missed one concert for you.'

The cruel, taunting words echoed over and over in Lauren's ears as she watched the girl turn and run back towards the hotel.

CHAPTER FIVE

THE sun was setting in a brilliant ball of orange that sent long fingers of colour stretching across the sea and sky. The palm trees were dark silhouettes against the blaze of colour and they swayed and rustled in the warm evening breeze.

The crew had worked for three hours in the intense heat of the afternoon and now, showered and refreshed, were sitting out on the terrace having drinks before dinner.

Lauren hesitated about joining them—she had deliberately kept out of everyone's way all afternoon. Since her talk with Donna she had been in no mood for further discussion.

Jon found her as she lingered by the doors leading out to the terrace. 'There you are. Did you hear about the commotion out by the gates today?' He launched into telling her about it in a heated manner that told her very clearly that Jon was not in the best of moods. That makes two of us, she thought morosely.

'They wouldn't let me in, can you believe that?' Dark eyes blazed down at her furiously. 'Said that only five musicians were booked in, and then when they saw a professional-looking camera around my neck they told me to step out of the car.'

'They have an aversion to members of the Press here, it seems,' Lauren said in a calm voice. 'The place is sacrosanct for the élite.'

'So I gather, but my money is as good as the next person's——' Jon broke off and then grinned as humour was quickly restored. 'Or should I say Warren's money? You know he's going to have a fit when he gets the bill for this place. We better bring back a good story or we are dead meat.'

'I know.' Lauren's gaze moved to the glass doors to watch the group again. Cole and Donna were talking with a couple she had never met before. Donna's hand was resting on Cole's arm in a possessive manner, and every now and then she slanted a look up at him that was almost coquettish.

'Well, one thing is for sure, Donna is definitely the bride-to-be,' Lauren murmured drily. 'I even got a glimpse of the wedding dress—well, a picture of it. She is having it specially made while we're here.'

'Now that is interesting news,' Jon grinned.

'Another bit of information I gleaned today is that Cole is quitting his career in music,' she added in a crisp, businesslike tone.

'Quitting?' Jon looked momentarily stunned. 'Are you sure about that?'

'Well... I have it from Donna. I'll have to check up with Cole before we can put it into print, but I'd say it's pretty certain.'

Jon rubbed his hands with glee. 'Warren is going to be well pleased with that juicy bit of information.'

'Yes, probably.' There was a lack of enthusiasm in her tone, but luckily Jon didn't notice.

He offered her his arm. 'Let's go and join them, then, shall we?'

For some reason she was glad of that arm as they walked out into the warmth of the evening. It was a shelter from Cole's dark, intense gaze, which seemed to burn through her as she walked towards him, reminding her of that kiss this afternoon.

The men around the table stood up as she reached them and Cole pulled out a chair next to him. 'Come and sit down, Lauren... Jon.' He added the other man's name as almost an afterthought. 'I'd like you to meet two very good friends of mine: Drew Sheldon, who is the owner of this hotel, and his wife, Amanda.'

Lauren smiled across at the other couple as she sat down next to Cole. The woman was about her own age and extremely attractive. Her hair was shoulder-length and a most magnificent shade of copper-gold. Her husband was a very handsome man; his hair was dark and just touched with a few strands of silver at his temples, which gave him a distinguished look.

'Very pleased to meet you.' He smiled across at her. 'Cole has spoken a lot about you.'

This nonplussed Lauren. What on earth would Cole have been talking about her for?

'Sorry again about this afternoon, Jon,' he said over to Jon, who was seated at the far end of the table.

He shrugged his shoulders good-naturedly.

'It's just that we like to guarantee complete privacy for our guests, and members of the Press——'

'Tend to make some people very nervous,' Jon finished for him with a grin. 'It's OK, I understand.'

A waiter arrived to take their order for drinks. 'Will you be eating out on the terrace, sir?' he asked Drew in perfect English.

Drew shot an enquiring glance at his wife. 'Let's eat back at our suite, Drew,' she said quickly. 'I shouldn't really be sitting out here at this hour of the day; the mosquitoes seem to love my fair skin.'

Drew shook his head and laughed. 'And that excuse is as good as any.' Catching Lauren's puzzled expression, he explained, 'We have a six-month-old baby, and although I employ a child-minder Amanda can't bear to be away from her for more than fifteen minutes at a time——'

'That's not true, Drew,' Amanda interrupted him with a laugh. 'I've been away a whole...' she glanced at her watch '... twenty minutes now.'

Everyone laughed. 'See what I mean?' Drew grinned.

Amanda rolled her eyes. 'Don't pretend you're any different. You can't bear to be away from her either.' She looked across at Cole and smiled. 'He was all set for taking her to a board meeting last Tuesday.'

'Well, she'll have a large empire to run one of these days, so you can't start educating her into the way of it soon enough.' Cole grinned.

'Exactly what I said.' Drew smiled. He glanced around the table. 'I hope you will all come and have dinner with us?'

The invitation was unanimously accepted.

Their private suite turned out to be a large bungalow-type building set apart and slightly back from the hotel. It was luxuriously furnished in a sophisticated style that seemed to suit the couple so well.

Dinner was a very relaxed and enjoyable occasion. Amanda and Drew were entertaining hosts and Lauren liked them both a great deal. Amanda, it turned out, was the Amanda Hunter of Hunter Fashions. Her designs had taken Paris by storm a couple of years ago and since then her name had become synonymous with sophisticated and elegant clothes.

'It's Amanda's boutique here in the hotel that's making up my dress for me,' Donna informed them as the dessert trolley was wheeled in filled with the most mouthwatering chocolate, cream and tropical fruit concoction that Lauren had ever seen. 'I have quite a few of Amanda's designs in my wardrobe. Well, anybody who is anybody has a Hunter dress.'

Amanda's lips curved in a gentle smile. 'I don't know if I quite agree with you there, but thank you for the compliment anyway.'

'Why don't you go in, Lauren, and get yourself something for the party tomorrow night?' Cole's eyes met hers directly across the table. 'A beautiful woman deserves to wear only the best.'

Lauren's heart thudded painfully at those words. He had said them to her so often in the past. She found herself remembering a shopping spree that he had taken her on in Beverly Hills. He had bought her so many new outfits and accessories that they had had to enlist the help of his chauffeur to carry them.

'If Lauren comes into the boutique in the morning, will you be able to fix her up with something special, Amanda?' he continued lightly.

'Of course I will.' Amanda smiled at her. 'I'll give it my personal attention.'

'Thank you.' Lauren didn't know what else to say. She carefully avoided Cole's eyes across the table. She was uncomfortable with the memories he had stirred up and also annoyed at the intimate tone of the conversation.

Her eyes collided with Donna. The other woman looked furious and Lauren didn't blame her. Didn't Cole realise that a personal comment like that would upset his fiancée?

Liqueurs and coffee were served in the large airy conservatory that led off the dining-room. Wicker furniture was placed strategically to catch the breathtaking view down over the beach now bathed with silver moonlight.

The men launched into a deep conversation about the music business and how it was changing—all except for Jon, that was. He was engaged in a quiet conversation with Donna. The faint sound of a baby's cry interrupted the relaxed atmosphere.

'That's Emma.' Amanda was on her feet immediately. 'If you'll excuse me, I'll just go and see to her.' She glanced down at Lauren. 'You're welcome to come and have a little peep at her if you like?'

Lauren nodded and stood up.

'You too, Donna?' Amanda included the other woman, who was still chatting with Jon.

'Er—no, I'll see her later,' she mumbled, and continued on with her conversation.

'Well, I'd like to take a little look, if you don't mind, Amanda?' Cole asserted. 'I haven't seen her yet.'

Lauren glanced across at him in surprise. Since when had Cole Adams been interested in babies? she wondered coolly. Maybe he was trying to cover up for Donna's rather abrupt refusal to even glance at the child?

A small night-light lit the nursery. A mobile of pink rabbits that hung over the cot sent shadows dancing over the white lace covers and the rows of soft toys that adorned the pretty room.

Amanda leaned over the cot, making low soothing noises, and lifted the child. Immediately the crying stopped. 'That's better.' Amanda kissed the little face. 'You just think you should have been invited for dinner too—that's the problem, isn't it?' She turned the baby so that they could see her properly. 'There, now, this is Miss Emma Sheldon.'

The most adorable large dark eyes stared over at them from a perfect little cherub face.

'Oh, she is beautiful,' Lauren said with a sigh.

'She certainly is.' Cole reached out a gentle hand and brushed back a little curl that was resting on her forehead. The child smiled up at him.

'She's in love with you already,' Amanda grinned. 'Six months old and already she has a smile for a handsome man. What is this power you have over women, Cole?'

'Damned if I know.' He grinned and slanted a wry glance at Lauren. 'I think you ought to be asking Lauren that.'

Lauren's eyebrows lifted. 'Might have something to do with the fact that you are an out-and-out... for the sake of Emma's ears I'll say rogue.'

Amanda laughed. 'You might have something there. The more heartache they give us, the more intrigued we become.'

'Until we grow up and learn better,' Lauren murmured.

Emma started to cry again. 'I think maybe she's hungry,' Amanda said, glancing down at her. 'I'll just go and put a bottle on—here...' She passed her to Lauren. 'Just hold on to her for a moment.'

It gave Lauren a strange feeling holding that small warm body close. Emma stopped crying again and stared up at her with trusting eyes.

If her pregnancy had gone full term she would have been holding her own baby now. She glanced over at Cole and met that dark gaze. If things had been different, it could have been like this for them. They could have been standing in a small nursery with their own child.

It was silly to think those kind of thoughts; she tried to banish the idea and the feelings it had aroused but it was hard, very hard when she felt that warm little body cuddling against her and the man she had loved so very much standing beside her. Panic rushed in a giant wave right through her. She wasn't going to cry, was she? Not here, not in front of Cole. 'Here.' Her hands shook as she held the child out to him. 'You hold her; she's a bit heavy.'

His eyes watched her steadily, but he said nothing, just took the child.

Then she turned away. 'I think I'll turn in for the night.'

She practically collided with Amanda in the doorway. 'Are you all right, Lauren?' she asked, putting a steadying hand on her arm, her eyes quizzical as they searched Lauren's pale features.

'Fine, just tired. I'm going to go back to the hotel now, Amanda, but thank you for a lovely evening.' She hoped her voice didn't sound as breathless as she felt. Suddenly she just wanted to be away from everyone.

'OK, I'll see you in the morning for your dress fitting,' Amanda said gently.

Lauren just nodded; she would have agreed to anything just to get out of there.

Her goodnights to Drew and the others were brief, almost clipped. Then she was outside and running, running as if all the devils in hell were after her.

When she stopped she was down on the beach and then she just slipped her sandals off and continued to walk.

The night air was hot; only the small breeze that was making the waves roll in and break with a surging crash against the shore stopped it from being unbearable. After a while she sat down and stared out across the moonlit sea. The night was so beautiful. There was silence except for the waves and the rustle of the palm trees. On a night like this it was hard to imagine that life could be bitter, that fate could be cruel.

She found herself remembering Cole's face when she had tried to tell him about her pregnancy. Harsh anger had been etched clearly across those handsome features. That look was a million miles away from the way he had tenderly taken Amanda's baby into his arms.

'I won't be bulldozed into making a commitment I'm not ready to make.' His stark words played and replayed through her mind. She tried to blank them out but they just wouldn't go away. How could he have thought her so calculating? He had lived with her for nearly a year and he hadn't known her at all.

* * *

For several nights she had slept in the room next to Cole's, thinking that he would come to her, that deep down he really loved her and needed her. That he hadn't meant those awful words.

Every morning she heard him leaving the house at dawn and he didn't return until nearly midnight. She had always been wide awake. She missed the warmth of his body next to hers, the way he had cradled her so tenderly in his arms. Cole was too busy to miss her.

Then one night, when he had arrived home at midnight, his footsteps had slowed as he came down the corridor and, instead of passing right by as they had done every other night, he had hesitated. Then the door had swung open.

'Are you awake?' His voice had sounded tense. His body was just a silhouette against the brightly lit hall.

She hadn't answered immediately, had just stared at his dark figure, her heart thudding wildly. Had he come to tell her that he was sorry for the things he had said; that he loved her?

'This is driving me crazy, Laurie.' His voice held a deep rasp, as if he was holding on to control by a mere thread. 'You know we can't go on like this.'

'I know.' Her voice was a mere whisper in the silence of the room.

He stretched out a hand and flicked on the bright overhead light. For a moment they just stared at each other. Then he moved into the room and sat down beside her on the edge of the bed. His eyes raked over her blonde hair spread silkily over the pillows, the paleness of her skin against the dark silk covers.

Silence stretched between them. His dark hair was ruffled as if he had been repeatedly raking his hands through it. The dark eyes held a kind of wildness that she had never seen in them before.

'Have... have you changed your mind about us?' She didn't know what else to say. Somehow the question didn't sound right; it sounded cold, like some kind of ultimatum. 'I'm not trying to trap you into anything, Cole.' Her voice was a husky whisper. 'If you want me to leave, then I'll go.' Her blue eyes misted with tears.

He swore under his breath. 'If you're trying to make me feel guilty, then you're doing a good job, Lauren.' He bent his head down towards her until his lips were only inches from hers. 'Don't turn on the tears, sweetheart.'

Icy disappointment flowed through her in waves, her lips quivered as the tears threatened to fall. He still thought that she was playing emotional roulette with him. 'What do you want from me, Cole?' She forced herself to ask the direct question, her voice low and tremulous.

'I want this.' His lips crushed down against hers in a powerful kiss. 'That's all that matters right now.'

Lauren struggled and twisted her head away. Immediately he released her and sat up. 'I want to make love to you, Laurie, but if you don't want me all you've got to do is say so and I'll go and leave you alone.' As he was speaking in that low, husky tone his hand was moving beneath the covers, his fingers running in a silky caress over the softness of her skin. Her head twisted around to stare up at him as his hand lingered against her breast.

'Just tell me you don't want me,' he invited in a low whisper.

Lauren's eyes filled with tears. In that moment she hated him, yet she loved him with an equal intensity. She couldn't tell him she didn't want him because it wasn't true—she did want him. She wanted him so much that it hurt.

A small triumphant smile curved his lips as he bent his head and once more took possession of her lips.

When she awoke the next morning in the cool light of dawn she was once more alone in that bed and she hated herself; she hated herself almost as much as she hated Cole.

She should never have allowed Cole to touch her—not after he had made things so clear. He didn't love her; he desired her. He wanted the warmth of her body but he didn't want her and he certainly wouldn't want this baby. Allowing him to stay with her last night had been wrong and she felt torn in two with guilt over it. It was almost as if she had had to make a choice between her baby and Cole, and last night she had placed her child second to her love for Cole. That fact disgusted her completely and she felt a surge of protective love towards her baby. What kind of a person was she, to have stayed with Cole after he had made it so clear that he wanted nothing but a casual affair?

Before she had time to think about where she was going or what she was doing, she got out of her bed, packed her bags and left without a backward glance, without even writing a letter of explanation. No words of explanation were necessary.

It took Cole a whole month to get in contact with her. Of course he was a busy man; he fitted in two short tours in that time. It was only when he got back to the ranch that he thought to call her. He must have had a rare spare moment on his hands and decided to give her a call. He hadn't even bothered to calculate the time back in London and it was nearly one in the morning when the phone shattered the silence of the night in Lauren's flat.

She wasn't asleep; she was staring into the darkness of her bedroom, tears of regret and self-recrimination flowing down her cheeks in never-ending rivulets.

'Lauren?' Hearing that warm, husky voice sent no wave of feeling through her; she felt cold, as if part of her body had ceased to function. 'Lauren, can we talk?'

Talk? Anger was then slowly unleashed. That he should ring her so calmly after a whole month and ask her casually, could he talk? The man had an unmitigated arrogant nerve; how dared he? 'Do you know it's one o'clock in the morning here?' she asked in an icy voice.

'Is it?' He sounded unconcerned, yet there was an undertone to his voice that told her he was tired, almost dropping with fatigue. Working too hard on his tours as usual, she thought with a sudden surge of bitterness.

'I'm sorry, Lauren. I just wanted to know how you are.'

'I'm wonderful, fine, ecstatic.' Her voice was choked with bitterness.

The silence at the other end of the line was so thick as to be almost a tangible force. 'Lauren, I——'

'Look, Cole, I've put my life back together now and there is no room in it for cosy little chats with you,' she cut across him in a voice that trembled alarmingly. 'So you see, you're off the hook. I wasn't out to trap you into making a commitment. I don't need you, I'm perfectly happy without you.'

'I need to see you, Lauren.' His voice was a husky drawl and she swallowed hard.

'Why?' Her hand tightened almost painfully around the receiver.

He gave a dry laugh. 'Because there are things we need to straighten out.'

She closed her eyes. 'There's nothing to straighten out, Cole. It's over, finished, and quite frankly you are the last person I need to see.' How she managed to sound so mocking when inside her heart was breaking she just didn't know. She rubbed a hand across her face, wiping the tears that were falling in a never-ending torrent.

'Laurie, honey, are you crying?' he asked gently into the silence.

She gave a small, bitter smile. They knew each other so well. She knew that he was raking his hand through his dark hair in the way he always did when he was impatient or annoyed about something. He knew that she was weeping her heart out.

'I'm catching the first plane out,' he said suddenly and unexpectedly. 'Hopefully I should be at your flat just after——'

'No,' she cut across him abruptly. 'I don't want to see you; I never want to see you again.'

'You don't mean that.' His voice was firm.

'Yes, I do. I mean it more than I've ever meant anything in all my life.' Then she calmly and coldly put down the receiver.

In her heart she knew that he would still come. When Cole made up his mind to do something he was never one to vary from that course.

It was no surprise when he turned up on her doorstep. What was a surprise was the way she felt towards him. There was no warm rush of feeling that had always accompanied meetings with him in the past. She felt totally cold towards him, indifferent almost, and that was very odd. Cole had always stirred up the most intense, extreme reaction in her. But now she didn't love him, she didn't hate him; she just felt nothing, as if part of her had died.

When he reached calmly to kiss her she turned her head away. 'I told you not to come.'

'I had to come. I have a responsibility to——'

'Responsibility!' She broke across him with a raw laugh. 'That's really rich, coming from you. I didn't think you knew that word existed.'

'Maybe I didn't until I met you,' he answered quietly. 'I've learnt quite a bit about myself, about you, over the last few weeks.'

'Well, bully for you.' She sat down in one of the old comfortable armchairs and stared up at his tall, powerful frame.

He looked down at her, his dark eyes serious and intent. 'I want you to come home with me.' He said the words so quietly that for a moment she thought she was hearing things. Then she just shook her head.

'I *am* home. This is where I belong. Warren has given me my old job back. I've been very lucky really.' She tilted her head in an almost defiant way. 'Like you, I've learnt quite a lot over the last few weeks, and one of those things is that I made a big mistake giving up my job to be with you.'

'Is that the bottom line, Lauren? Is that why you left?'

She stared up at those bleak dark features and something inside her just snapped. 'I left because I was carrying your baby and you had made it perfectly clear that you didn't want me.' She hadn't intended to tell him; there didn't seem any point in telling him, but she just couldn't keep the pain and the hurt bottled up inside her any longer. She wanted to accuse him, she wanted him to feel some of the guilt that was wedged deep inside her.

He stared at her incredulously. 'You're pregnant!' his voice grated roughly. 'Why the hell——?'

'Correction, Cole. I *was* pregnant,' she cut across him before he could say any more, then looked away from him, swallowing hard. She wasn't going to cry, she told herself fiercely. She had shed enough tears this last couple of weeks to last a lifetime.

For a moment the silence in the room was almost a tangible force. 'You mean you had a termination?' The question was asked in a low, raw tone that made her flinch.

She moved from the chair and crossed the room so her back was towards him. She couldn't handle this; she didn't want him to see her lose control and she was holding on to it by a mere whisper.

'Answer me, Lauren.' A rough hand on her shoulder whirled her around to face him. He looked furious, his dark face etched with grim lines.

'I had a miscarriage two weeks ago.' She told him the truth quietly, tears shimmering in her blue eyes.

His hand dropped from her arm. 'I see.' There was a gentle note in his voice now that tore at her heart. 'You should have told me, Lauren. I——'

'And what would you have done, Cole?' she asked furiously. 'Sympathised? Said, "Never mind, it's for the best"? As I said before, you're off the hook. Don't pretend to be sorry.'

'Maybe I don't want to be off the hook,' he said quietly.

'Don't insult my intelligence, Cole.' Her eyes flashed fire at him. 'If there is one thing that I've learnt recently it's just how wrong I was to get involved with you. We're going in opposite directions in life, we want different things. Our affair was doomed from the start.'

'That's not true, Lauren.' He raked a hand through thick dark hair. 'Look, get changed and I'll take you out to dinner. We'll talk about everything, about the baby——'

'It's too late to talk,' she said calmly.

'God damn it, it's never too late.' His calm control snapped.

'Yes, it is, Cole.' She looked up at him with clear blue eyes. 'It's too late for our baby and it's way, way too late for us...'

* * *

'Lauren.' The voice interrupted her thoughts and, startled, she looked up to see Cole standing beside her. 'Are you OK?'

'I was,' she answered drily.

He ignored the sarcasm and sat down beside her on the soft powdery white sand. There was silence for a while as they both stared out at the sea, both in their own private world of thoughts.

'What do you want, Cole?' she asked at last.

'Do I have to want something before I can come and sit next to you?' he asked, a slight edge to his tone now. 'As a matter of fact I was just taking a stroll before turning in for the night when I happened to see you.'

'Well, why don't you just stroll on by?' Her voice was abrasive; she felt angry for some reason. Maybe it was the powerful intensity of her memories.

She knew her words had angered him—she could feel the tension between them in the air, but he didn't say anything to retaliate; instead he said gently, 'Amanda was rather concerned about you when you left so abruptly.'

'Well, I'm sorry if I upset her,' she said shortly. 'I just needed to be on my own for a little while.'

He didn't take the hint and leave as she had hoped. Instead he leaned back on his elbows and stared up at the sky. 'Have you noticed,' he said idly, 'that the moon is hanging upside-down in the sky?'

She glanced upwards, startled by the sudden observation. She had noticed earlier how the silver crescent-shaped moon was lying on its back as if it had slipped drunkenly off its perch. 'Maybe we're just looking at it from a different angle.' She tilted her head sideways. 'Do you think in London we look at it sideways on?'

'Or maybe in the busy, hectic whirl of our lives we don't have time to stop and look at it at all.' His voice was tinged with regret. 'Strange, isn't it, how different things can look when viewed from another angle?' His tone was reflective and she knew he was talking about things other than the moon.

She slanted a glance at him and their eyes locked. 'When I saw you holding that baby this evening something just seemed to hit me, right there.' He placed a hand against the flat planes of his stomach.

For a moment she could only stare at him in surprise. Then he reached out that hand towards her and she flinched away.

'I'm sorry, Lauren.' He allowed the hand to drop on to the sand. 'I don't think I told you just how sorry, when I came to see you in London, after... after it had happened.'

She wanted to make some kind of a sarcastic, cutting reply but none came to her lips; her breath seemed to freeze along with her thoughts.

'You know, when I came to see you that last time in London and I gave you that ultimatum to come back with me to California...' His voice trailed off and for a moment he seemed a million miles away. 'I actually went to talk with your doctor afterwards.'

Her eyes widened with shock as she swung to face him. 'What on earth...?'

'I know it was crazy.' He shrugged broad shoulders. 'But I would have done anything at that point; I just felt so bad about everything.'

'You mean you felt guilty,' she said, and her voice was cracked and harsh again now.

'Maybe.' Again he shrugged. 'We all have moments of guilt in our lives; I don't suppose any of us are perfect. Looking back, I think that you and I have had more than our fair share of guilt and regret.' His eyes sought hers and held them steadily. 'Yet it wasn't our fault, Lauren.'

'No?' She swallowed hard. 'Then whose fault was it?' she asked with bitter contempt. 'The man in the moon?'

'Does it have to be someone's fault?' he answered calmly. 'It was one of those things——'

'Losing a baby is not *just one of those things*.' She flung the words at him contemptuously. 'You wouldn't understand in a million years how I felt inside...' Her voice shook with a rush of bitter emotion. 'The acute sense of loss, the remorse... I still feel it so deeply.'

'But it wasn't anyone's fault, Lauren. You had a miscarriage, the doctor said that sometimes that is nature's way——'

'I know what the doctor said,' she snapped in a brittle tone. 'But maybe if I hadn't made that journey from California to London it would never have happened—maybe it's all my fault.'

'No, you're talking rubbish.' He reached out and took her hand. 'You aren't to blame for what happened; you're going to have to stop torturing yourself with those thoughts.'

She shook her head and one teardrop rolled slowly down the smooth paleness of her cheek. 'But I wanted that baby so much, Cole.'

There was heavy silence for a moment. Lauren, lost in her thoughts, was only vaguely aware of the stroking movement of Cole's hand against the warm skin of her arm.

'There will be other babies. You're young and——'

'Save your words of sympathy, Cole, they ring very hollowly in my ears,' she cut across him bitterly, and pulled her arm roughly away from his grasp. 'Don't pretend that you give a damn, because I know you don't.'

'That's not true.' His voice held a deep patient tone as if he were explaining something to a child. 'I never meant to hurt you, Lauren. What happened between us was a mistake——'

'You can say that again,' she cut across him with bitter sarcasm, but she was surprised to find how much it hurt to hear him talk about their relationship like that. 'And it's a mistake I want to forget. I certainly don't want to talk about it.'

'I think you *need* to talk about it,' he said firmly and with an arrogance that made her blood boil. 'It's the only way to put it behind you, then you'll be able to start afresh.'

She remembered with brooding bitterness how Donna had told her that Cole felt sorry for her. Was that the reason he was out here talking to her like this? Was that the reason she had been asked out to Thailand? She brushed an impatient hand over her tear-stained face, her lips tightened in an angry line. She didn't need his concern or his pity; she was nobody's fool. 'This may come as a surprise to you, Cole, but I am a tough, independent career-woman, not a simpering emotional wreck. Sorry to disappoint you, but I have succeeded in starting afresh without your counselling.'

'Am I to take it, then, that you've decided to dedicate your life to your career?' he asked drily.

Her eyes narrowed on him. 'You sound disapproving, which I find strange seeing as you've spent the last few years doing exactly that. You're not going to tell me that it's all right for a man to be dedicated to his career but not a woman, are you?' she asked contemptuously.

'No, I'm not going to try and tell you that.' His lips twisted sardonically. 'I just happen to think that you're the type of woman who needs more from life than her career.'

'Is there anything more important than a career?' She tossed the question at him flippantly.

'How about a husband, a family?' The gravel-deep tone cut the silence around her like shock waves reverberating over and over with painful intensity. 'There was a point during our relationship when that was what you wanted, wasn't there?'

She swallowed hard, hating the arrogant ease with which he was able to ask questions like that. 'There was, yes.' With difficulty she kept her voice steady. 'Then I realised when I got home to England that I had very nearly made the worst mistake of my life. That I had wanted those things from the wrong man.'

'And do you honestly imagine that Jon is the right man for you?' He asked the question with scathing contempt.

She frowned at that question. 'Jon and I have a lot in common, we work well together, he's a nice guy, but——'

'And since when has "nice" been a recommendation for falling in love?' he drawled scornfully. 'You do realise that you've fallen for Jon on the rebound?'

Lauren stared at him in angry amazement. 'And just what is that remark supposed to mean?'

'Just what I said.' His mouth set in a firm line.

'You really believe that because we broke up I went out and flung myself into the arms of the first available man?' she demanded, incensed by such an arrogant assumption.

'Something like that,' he agreed easily.

'You really are the most conceited man I've ever met,' she muttered furiously.

'I don't think that that's conceit...concern is a more apt name for it I'd say.'

'So, you're concerned about me...how touching,' she lashed out at him with a honeyed tone. How dared he patronise her as if she were some dim-witted child?

'You're not in love with him, Lauren. You're kidding yourself if you think you are.' His voice was supremely confident and it made Lauren's blood boil. 'You've been through a traumatic time and it's natural that you might want to take refuge in the nearest pair of comforting arms, but, take it from me, Jon will never make you happy.'

'Well, thank you for the psychoanalysis, Dr Adams,' she grated scornfully.

'Any time.' He grinned at her with easy good humour. 'And it's all completely free of charge.'

Her hands clenched at his infuriating attitude and all she could think of was wiping that arrogant smile off his face. 'You think you know me so well, don't you, Cole?' she said in a shaking voice.

'I think I do, yes.' There was no hesitation; his dark eyes rested on the vulnerable curve of her lips. 'You shared my bed for a long while. I think I know what turns you on, and what doesn't. Jon is not for you.'

Her face flared with red-hot heat. How dared he speak to her like that? She itched to take him down a peg, to tell him how wrong he was, to hurt him the way he was hurting her.

'You are so wrong, Cole.' He had goaded her too far and now all she could think of was lashing out. It didn't matter that it was a downright lie that tripped off her tongue as long as she struck back at him. 'You see, I've never been happier than I am with Jon.' She got lightly up on to her feet and brushed an absent hand at the sand on the blue silk dress. 'He's a gentle, caring man, and that's something that I've learnt to appreciate after the coldness I experienced with you.'

Cole also rose to his feet. She slanted a quick look at him and then promptly wished she hadn't. The grim expression on that dark face was positively frightening. 'Our relationship could be described as a lot of things, but cold is not one of them.' There was a jeering, sardonic note in his voice now, one that sent a shiver of apprehension racing down her spine. 'In fact, I would describe the way you used to respond to me as passionately hot.'

She flinched at those words and at the tone with which they were delivered. She supposed she had asked for his anger—she had struck a blow to his male ego; but that he should be so cruel, so insensitive as to keep reminding her of how totally she had given herself to him seemed brutally harsh.

'That comment was beneath contempt,' she told him in a low, furious tone. 'You will never be half the gentleman that Jon Richards is.'

He shrugged, completely impervious to the remark. 'And you will never respond to Richards the way you once responded to me. Whether you want to admit it or not, there was once a time when I only had to glance at you to set you on fire.'

Her heart hammered as if it were about to explode at those words. He was the most arrogant, contemptible man she had ever met. 'If you were a lighted torch you couldn't set me on fire,' she informed him in a lofty tone, her head held high. Then she turned and walked with as much dignity and pride as she could muster away from him.

'That sounds dangerously like a challenge, Lauren.' The softly spoken words fell into the heat of the night, like a cool breeze before the storm.

His hand on her arm came as a surprise; she hadn't heard his footsteps following her on the softness of the sand. He wheeled her around in a manner that was none too gentle.

'What on earth are you doing?' She struggled to remove his hand from her arm but it was like a tight band of steel.

'I'm proving something to you,' he grated harshly.

She watched the slow descent of his head towards hers with a kind of numb disbelief. All right, so she had insulted his macho pride, but there was no excuse for this outrageous behaviour.

'Stop it, Cole!' She put her hand up against the smooth silk of his shirt.

His lips touched hers. The warm, firm pressure against her softness sent an electric current of sensation shooting right down to her toes. She forced herself to remain perfectly still. She wouldn't respond to him; she would show him just how impervious she was to his caresses.

His hand left her arm to curve around her waist and suddenly he had pulled her roughly in against the heat of his body. His other hand wound up through the silky curls of her hair, holding her as the pressure of his mouth intensified.

Lauren's heart slammed in heavy painful beats against her chest, making her feel as if her whole body was getting ready to explode. The kiss was hard and punishing and she refused to respond to it. Then it slowed and his lips moved in a deeply sensuous way. Against her will she could feel herself starting to relax against him now. He was a skilled lover and he knew her lips and her body so well.

'Hell, Lauren, you feel so good.' The husky drawl of his voice against her skin sent shivers racing down her spine. From nowhere heat and desire spiralled up in a torrent of feeling to her lips, her arms curved upwards against his broad chest, and she was returning his kisses with a wild abandonment that was completely out of control. She had forgotten everything except the pleasure of being in his arms.

Even after he had pulled back from her, she continued to cling to him, her thoughts incoherent.

'Not a bad response for someone who claimed to be immune to my charms.' The husky words had an arrogant ring, as if he was smugly pleased. 'Now try telling me that you respond to Jon like that.'

It took a moment before his words penetrated the mists of passion that had distorted her thinking. Then she stepped back. Her eyes were glazed with tears of bewilderment and anger as she stared up at his dark face. 'I hate you, Cole Adams,' she whispered in a voice that trembled with emotion.

One eyebrow lifted sardonically. 'I can live with your hatred, Lauren Martin,' he replied easily.

CHAPTER SIX

THAT night seemed never-ending. Lauren tossed and turned, and even though the room was cool from the air-conditioning system she felt hot, almost feverish.

She kept remembering the way Cole had kissed her, the way she had responded to him, and her temperature seemed to increase still further. Why had she allowed herself to respond like that? Especially as she had known he was just proving a point. Where was the professionally cool attitude that she had vowed she would maintain around him?

She wished she were a million miles away from Cole and this whole situation. She didn't want to attend his wedding, she didn't want to watch him exchange vows with Donna. She didn't want him to marry Donna. The thought hit her out of nowhere.

Angry with herself, she turned her head into her pillow. She needed to get some sleep; if she just managed to get a couple of hours she would be able to put all this in perspective tomorrow. She certainly wasn't thinking rationally now.

She closed her eyes and the memory of that kiss was even stronger. Then she found herself remembering other things, the way Cole used to hold her, the way he had once made love to her. The memories crowded forcefully into her mind until her body ached with the anguish of them. What on earth was the matter with her? she wondered furiously. She was being utterly ridiculous.

The next thing she remembered was someone knocking on the door.

'Lauren, are you awake? It's eight o'clock.' It was Jon's voice, and with a sigh she got up to let him in.

'Good morning.' He breezed in and his eyes flicked over her slender figure in the silk kimono. 'How come you look so sexy first thing in the morning?' he demanded with a good-natured grin, his eyes lingering on the softness of her lips.

'Flattery will get you absolutely nowhere,' Lauren told him with a smile.

'I know, but you can't blame a guy for trying,' he said, a wicked gleam in his eye.

Lauren had to laugh. 'I think Cole's right about you. You are a dreadful flirt.'

'I don't mind being labelled a flirt,' Jon said with a shrug. 'But I don't want to be labelled a dreadful one.' He went and stood next to her dressing-table and studied his reflection in the mirror as he spoke to her. 'Everyone is getting ready to leave for Phang Nga for the day. They are going to shoot the remaining scenes for the video out there. That's where they shot the James Bond movie, *Man with the Golden Gun*, you know.' He picked up her comb and neatened his thick blond hair with a few careful strokes. 'Donna told me that last night. It was a very enjoyable evening, wasn't it?'

'Was it?' Lauren sat down in the chair beside him and hoped he hadn't noticed how flat her voice sounded.

'You don't sound too enthusiastic.' He glanced down at her. 'Everything all right?'

'Of course.' She forced a brightness into her tone that she wasn't really feeling. 'Just a little tired. I must admit that the thought of trailing after Cole and his entourage today is not exactly filling me with enthusiasm.'

'Well, why don't you take it easy today and just hang around the hotel? I'll take all the photos and keep my ears open in case there are any interesting developments,' Jon suggested easily.

The suggestion was tempting, very tempting. Lauren really didn't feel in the mood for Cole's and Donna's company. Not after her exchange with Cole on the beach last night.

'I think one of us should be around to ring Warren today anyway,' Jon continued. 'He'll want to know what's going on.'

Lauren nodded and relief swept through her. 'Yes, you're right.'

'OK, I'll see you later on, then.' Jon moved towards the door. 'Try and get some rest, Lauren,' he said before closing the door behind him.

Her eyes moved briefly towards her reflection in the dressing-table mirror. She was still so pale, she thought as her eyes lingered on her lips before she turned angrily away. Damn Cole Adams; she didn't know what she had been thinking about last night, to get so upset about his marriage to Donna. The woman was welcome to him. Strange how the mind could play tricks on you in the silence of the night. For a while there she could almost have believed she was still in love with him—which of course was complete nonsense.

Her mind ran back over her conversation with Cole and she found herself cringing when she remembered the deliberate lie about her relationship with Jon. Maybe she should have warned Jon about what she had said, for God alone knew what Cole might say to him today.

Quickly she got up from her seat and rushed towards the door, hoping to catch him while he was standing waiting for the lifts just down the corridor.

'Jon!' She called his name as soon as she opened her door, and was then mortified to find that he was not there and that the only person standing waiting for the lift was Cole. He turned as she called and his eyes moved briefly over her state of undress, the white silk kimono, the tousled blonde hair, the anxious light in her beautiful eyes.

'He's gone,' he informed her drily. 'Was it important?'

She shifted awkwardly. 'Er—no, it will do later. I just wanted to tell him something.'

'Something you forgot to tell him last night?' His tone was clipped and dry. 'Would you like me to pass on a message?'

'Er—no... no, thank you.' Embarrassed now, she started to retreat and close the door.

'Not something I could relate, hmm?' His tone was a long way off being pleasant. 'Lauren.' The crisp authoritative voice had no problem in detaining her. 'You are making a big mistake getting involved with Richards. A big, big mistake.'

'What the hell would you know about it?' For a moment their eyes met and held, both hostile, both intent on proving a point.

'You may have made love with Richards last night, but you aren't *in* love with him; that much is blatantly obvious.'

The taunting, sardonic comment brought a dull flush of colour to her cheeks. Before she could think of a suitably cutting reply the lift doors had opened and he had stepped inside, leaving her staring down an empty corridor.

Of all the arrogant nerve! She returned to her room and leaned back against the door angrily. Did he assume because she had returned one kiss that she was still infatuated by him? That man had one almighty ego.

Irately she dismissed the whole thing. She didn't give a damn about Cole Adams, she told herself, and went into the bathroom to run herself a bath. She was going to have a nice relaxing day and she wasn't going to spare the infuriating man one thought.

She had breakfast in her room and then on impulse wandered down to Amanda's boutique. She needed cheering up, and what better way than a new dress?

Everything about the Hunter Boutique spoke of extreme opulence, from the gold-embossed initials on the glass doors to the crystal chandeliers and deep red carpets. This was a place where only the beautiful people shopped.

Amanda arrived in as she was speaking with one of the assistants, and took over. 'Lauren, I'm glad you came in—I have just the dress for you,' she said with a smile, and disappeared back into her workshop for a moment. She reappeared a few seconds later. 'Here we are. Now give me a call when you have it on; I'm dying to see it on you.'

It was the kind of dress that looked deceptively simple on the hanger and then, when you stepped into it, transformed itself dramatically into an incredibly sensual and delectable creation.

The heavy black Thai silk had a deep watermark pattern that gleamed seductively as the light hit it; it was the perfect foil for Lauren's translucent creamy complexion and it showed the slender curves of her body to tantalising perfection.

'Wow!' Amanda's eyes lit up as she came back into the room a few moments later and surveyed her. 'I knew it would be right for you, but I don't think I envisaged just how right. You look spectacular!'

Lauren smiled and swung to look at herself in the gilt-edged mirrors. 'I don't think I've ever had such a beautiful dress,' she murmured reflectively. 'Even when I was living... out in California.' She had been about to say living with Cole.

She bit her lip and frowned as memories crowded her mind unexpectedly. Memories of how Cole had once spoilt her, how gentle and indulgent he had once been where she was concerned.

It was strange how recollections of her time with Cole could suddenly hit her when she was least expecting them, turning a happy moment into an extremely painful one. He had been so wonderful, generous, tender. Why had it all turned so disastrously wrong?

'Lauren?' Amanda's concerned voice pulled her away from the intense thoughts, and she turned with a smile that was a mere shadow of what it had previously been.

'Sorry, Amanda, I was miles away.' She whirled around and studied her reflection again. 'I love this dress,' she murmured, suddenly making up her mind to have it. Her confidence could do with the boost, especially for the party this evening.

They heard the door opening into the shop and Amanda excused herself for a moment to go and see who it was.

'Cole! I thought you had disappeared off to Phang Nga by now.'

'I've let them go on ahead. I have a little bit of business to attend to.'

Lauren could hear the deep, attractive tone clearly from where she stood in the fitting-room, and it made her heart pound. She had wanted to keep out of Cole's way today and yet there was this disturbing sensation of pleasure at just hearing his voice.

'I thought I'd pay you now for my suit and Donna's dress. Hopefully we should have things wrapped up this afternoon, which means definitely leaving tomorrow.'

The small bubble of pleasure evaporated completely at those words. He was settling the account for their wedding outfits and they were leaving tomorrow. Which meant their wedding could be only days away. Her heartbeat increased dramatically and painfully against her chest at the thought.

'Well, we'll be sorry to see you go, Cole,' Amanda was saying regretfully. 'But we still have this party to look forward to tonight. Actually you're just in time to have a sneak preview of Lauren's dress. She's in the fitting-room now. You can give us your opinion.'

Lauren cringed at the very thought of going out there and parading in front of him, and she hastily reached for the buttons of her dress to get out of it quickly.

She wasn't quick enough. Amanda returned to her before she had even unfastened the first one.

'Good, you've still got it on.' Amanda smiled at her. 'Cole's in the shop—come and show him.' She didn't give Lauren a chance to make an excuse but caught hold of her hand and led her through into the boutique.

He was leaning against the counter, looking very much at ease with the situation, unlike Lauren, who was dying a million deaths inside.

'Doesn't she look beautiful?' Amanda asked, a note of satisfaction in her voice. 'That dress could have been designed especially for Lauren, it looks so good.'

'It certainly does,' Cole agreed lazily. His dark eyes moved slowly from the tip of her toes up over her slender body, taking in its every curve and then lingering on the delicate face flushed with the heat of embarrassment.

'Turn around, Lauren, let's see the back,' he commanded.

She wanted to refuse, she wanted to race back to the sanctuary of the fitting-rooms. The way he was looking her over made her heart slam fiercely against her ribs. This reminded her of shopping trips of the past, how he had liked to help her choose her clothes, how he had liked to help her out of them when they were back in the privacy of their bedroom.

Determinedly she raised her chin. She wasn't going to allow herself to think like that. She gave a quick twirl, feeling the soft rustle of the silk as it swirled against her legs.

'Very, very lovely,' he drawled softly as she came around to face him. 'I'd say you're going to need some help with all those buttons, though, when it comes to getting out of it,' he added with a gleam in his dark eyes.

Lauren's face flushed a vivid scarlet at those teasing words. He had no right to make comments like that.

Amanda laughed, obviously unaware of the tension that was crackling inside Lauren. 'Men,' she said with amused derision. 'We spend so much time and effort wondering what to wear for them and all they can think about is how they can get us out of it.'

Lauren dragged her eyes away from Cole's dark gaze. 'Oh, I don't agree with you there, Amanda,' she said lightly. 'I've never dressed to please a man in my life. I dress to please myself.'

'I don't know about that, Lauren,' Cole said drily. 'I can remember a little black number of yours that you used to wear for me because I liked it.'

Lauren's eyes swung back to his and they blazed with fury. How dared he remind her of that? 'I think you have a memory that verges on the fanciful,' she said icily.

'Mmm... and you *were*, in that dress, as I recall,' he drawled smoothly. 'Very fanciable.'

Amanda laughed at that but Lauren found it singularly unamusing; in fact it just made her blood boil more than ever.

'Come on, you two, kiss and make up,' Amanda said in a lightly humorous tone.

'We did that last night,' Cole murmured drily. 'Well, we kissed, but unfortunately making up seems a little harder than I had envisaged.'

Lauren shook her head helplessly at such mockery. Just who did he think he was? He was a man on the verge of matrimony, he had just come in to pay for his wedding outfits, for heaven's sake, and here he was calmly raking back over their past affair and flirting outrageously. The man had no scruples whatsoever.

She turned her head disdainfully away from him and spoke to Amanda, pointedly ignoring him. 'I'll just go and take this dress off.'

'Shout if you need a hand,' Cole called after her, an amused note in the deep voice.

She ignored the gibe and walked with her head held high back into the fitting-room. The man was a monster, an ogre, she thought furiously.

She returned a little while later to the outside shop dressed once more in her primrose-yellow sundress, only to find that he was still there. In fact he looked as if he was waiting for her, because he was sitting patiently in one of the deep red armchairs, his arms folded across his broad chest, his long legs stretched out lazily in front of him.

She tried not to look at him but she could feel his dark eyes watching her every movement from the fitting-rooms to the counter.

Amanda was now talking to another client who had entered the boutique so Lauren handed the silk dress to her assistant for it to be wrapped.

She wished she didn't feel so self-conscious as she stood there waiting for the girl to finish. She wished that she couldn't feel those eyes boring straight into her back. She opened her handbag and took out her credit card ready to pay the girl as she handed the gold box across to her.

The girl looked at the credit card blankly. 'Your account has already been settled, Miss Martin,' she said with finality, pushing the card back to her.

Lauren shook her head. 'No...you've made a mistake. I haven't paid you yet.'

'I paid for the dress,' Cole's voice came clearly from behind.

'You did what?' She swung around to face him, her eyes blazing.

'I said, I paid for the dress,' Cole repeated calmly. 'It was the least I could do after teasing you so mercilessly.'

She shook her head wordlessly, fury shimmering in her bright blue eyes. How dared he patronise her in this manner? 'I...I'd rather you didn't,' she murmured in a low undertone. 'I'm perfectly capable of buying my own clothes.'

'I'm sure you are.' Humour gleamed behind his words. 'It's just a dress, Lauren, don't get so worked up. I've bought enough of them for you in the past.'

In one fell stroke he had succeeded in making her feel totally humiliated, and she positively hated him for it.

Leaving the dress box on the counter, she marched out of the shop, her head held high. She didn't want the damn dress, not if he'd paid for it. He had just gone too far with his arrogant sense of humour. There was something positively sordid about a man who bought his wife's wedding dress and his ex-mistress a party dress at one and the same time.

She walked mindlessly out through the Reception and then out of the side-doors into the gardens.

'And just where do you think you are going?' Cole's arm on her shoulder made her jump.

'For a walk—it's not illegal, is it?'

'No.' He pulled her forcibly to a standstill and turned her around to face him. 'But displays of temper are severely frowned upon out here,' he said drolly.

'I'm not displaying any temper; I'm walking quietly...by myself.' She met his gaze with eyes that glittered furiously.

The firm lips twisted in an arrogantly amused smile. 'Ever since you've arrived here you have been displaying temper,' he said.

'I have not!' she exclaimed heatedly. 'I've come to do a job, and if you'd just let me get on with it I'd be perfectly happy.'

He nodded. 'So why are you out here stomping around the gardens when you should be out at Phang Nga keeping an eye on the proceedings?'

'I'm not stomping anywhere. I'm waiting around so that I can phone Warren later.'

He glanced at his wristwatch and grinned. 'You'll have quite a wait. It won't be worth phoning England until at least four-thirty, unless you fancy waking him up in the middle of the night.'

'Well, I'll phone him up at four-thirty.'

'Which means you have time to come out to Phang Nga now with me.'

She shook her head helplessly. She didn't want to go anywhere with him... she just wanted to be as far away from him as she could possibly get.

'I'm just waiting for the chopper and we'll leave.'

'Chopper?' She looked at him in bewilderment.

'Helicopter,' he said with dry amusement. 'You know, one of those flying machines with large propellers.'

'Ha, ha,' she said acidly. 'Very funny.'

'Well, it might have been if you hadn't lost your sense of humour.' He took hold of her arm and led her over to where some chairs were placed under a pretty parasol by the swimming-pool. 'Come on, Lauren... we used to get on so well together. Why is it that I can't tease you any more without having my head bitten off... why do you insist on hating me?'

'I don't hate you.' She sat on the edge of the chair and looked out over the sparkling blue of the pool.

'Strange—you did last night,' he murmured, a gleam of amusement in the deep voice.

She turned her head towards him in annoyance. Why had she said that? Of course she hated him... she had meant that when she had said it last night.

Their eyes met and held. For a moment she thought she saw a look of tenderness in those deep eyes as they moved over the softness of her face. She looked away quickly again. Of course there was no tenderness in that gaze—he loved Donna, she told herself furiously.

'I just don't think it's appropriate for you to be teasing me, or buying me clothes, or anything else,' she said crisply.

'Because you don't want to upset your new boyfriend?' There was a sarcastic cutting edge to the tone now. 'You worry too much, Lauren. I really don't think anyone will read anything untoward in our being friendly.'

She shook her head. 'I'd hardly call that kiss last night just being friendly,' she murmured, then promptly wished she hadn't said that. She didn't want even to think about that kiss, let alone talk about it. 'And that dress is far too expensive a gift for any friend to buy.'

He gave a dry laugh at that. 'Not this friend,' he told her softly. 'You could have a hundred just like it if you wanted; it's nothing.'

'Well, it is to me,' she insisted firmly.

There was silence for a moment. 'All right. Maybe I went a bit far kissing you last night. I suppose I still find you attractive, and you did goad me.'

Her heart hammered unmercifully against her breast as she turned to look at him.

'Will you accept an apology?' he asked now.

For a moment she was so startled that she was lost for words. Cole was actually apologising. Among the surprise of that there was a kind of sinking feeling of disappointment that puzzled her intensely. Why should she feel disappointed by his apology? He had behaved abominably, kissing her like that when he was engaged to another woman, and it was only right that he should apologise.

'Well?' he prompted. 'Is my apology acceptable?'

She nodded and for a second couldn't find her voice. She felt choked by some emotion she didn't understand as she looked at the ruggedly handsome contours of his face. What was it about this man that seemed to churn her up inside?

'And as for the dress,' he continued on blithely, 'I want you to have it. From one friend to another, with love.'

She swallowed hard and for a moment a million emotions mixed and swirled inside her. Of course he was just trying to be kind now; why that kindness should make her want to cry she had no idea. Angrily she clenched her hands tightly together in her lap. She didn't want him to start being kind.

The noise of a helicopter's engine cut the silence of the afternoon and Cole glanced up into the clear blue of the sky. 'Well, looks as if it's time to go back to work,' he said easily as he got to his feet.

Lauren watched him walk a few feet away from her to stand and watch the aircraft land on the lawn behind them.

As far as he was concerned, the subject was over now, they were friends and he could get on with his work and with his fiancée, his mind content that he had done the right thing by her.

Her eyes moved over his broad-shouldered frame. He looked incredibly attractive in a pair of faded jeans and a white T-shirt that emphasised his dark hair and the mahogany sheen of his skin. He put up a hand and raked it through the thick dark hair as the breeze from the propellers ruffled it. Her hands tightened even more. What on earth was wrong with her? she wondered desperately. Why did she want to run across to him and put her hand in his? Why was she consumed by these intense mixed-up emotions every time she was close to him?

The pilot cut the engines of the helicopter and the noise faded as the blades slowed down. He got out and went across to speak to Cole.

'OK, Lauren.' Cole turned towards her as she started to get to her feet. 'We're ready to leave now.' He held a hand out towards her and for a second she hesitated.

'Come on, come on,' he said briskly. 'We haven't got all day.'

She walked across towards him with a shrug. He was so bossy, domineering, overbearing.

He grinned at her as she reached his side. 'That's better. I was beginning to think I'd lost the knack of how to handle you.'

She frowned and opened her mouth to tell him what she thought about such a chauvinistic statement. But before she could say anything he placed a hand over her lips.

'We don't want any angry words, thank you.' Then he ruffled her hair. 'Come on, let's go. The crew will be wondering where we've got to, and I want to have this wrapped up today.' He caught hold of her hand and led her towards the helicopter. It was just a casual hand, it meant nothing, yet it made Lauren's heart flutter.

He saw her into the front seat and strapped her in safely with deft fingers, then he climbed up beside her and started the engines.

Cole was a good pilot; he handled the controls deftly and with supreme confidence. Lauren relaxed back and watched him for a while as he manoeuvred the machine up and then turned it so that it flew down over the beach and out along the coast.

He turned and caught her watching him and smiled. 'Great scenery, isn't it?' He practically had to shout above the din of the engine.

She nodded and turned her eyes down towards the turquoise blue of the sea and the white beaches fringed with palm trees. It was beautiful—very natural and unspoilt.

After a while they were heading out over the mangroves towards scenery that reminded Lauren of Oriental paintings. Round mountain-tops poked from the blue waters, some had their own beaches around them, others were just sheer limestone rocks that rose steeply like dark fingers pointing up from the sparkling waters towards the vivid blue sky.

'There they are.' Cole pointed down towards one of the islands and Lauren could see the crew standing on the smooth white sand. Some of them looked up as they heard the engine, and waved.

Cole grinned at Lauren. 'Well, I guess now that they've spotted us we will have to put this baby down. Shame really—I was almost tempted to whisk you off to Phi Phi island and spend the day just lounging on the beach with you.'

She shook her head, not believing that for one moment. 'What, and let work take a back seat? That would never do, Cole. What on earth would Donna say?'

He shrugged. 'I don't know what she would say. I don't expect she'd be too pleased. We're shooting the end of her solo number today.'

As he was speaking he was taking the aircraft down towards the beach. 'And anyway, I'll have enough time to lounge around as soon as I get this finished. Work is definitely taking a back seat then. I want to take it easy for a while, enjoy life a bit.'

She turned to look at him. 'So it is true that you intend to give up your singing career?'

'Who told you that?' He frowned and then his brow cleared. 'Donna, I suppose?'

She nodded.

'She never could keep a secret,' he muttered drily.

'So it's true?' she persisted, her eyes moving over the rugged contours of his face. For some reason she really wanted him to deny it.

Instead he flashed her that white smile of his. 'Yes, it's true. I'm finally ready to stop all the tours and settle down. Shocking, isn't it?'

'Totally.' She agreed with him in the same light-hearted tone as he had used, but inside she felt totally despondent. Why was it that part of her had hoped Donna was spinning her a line? 'Amazing what love will do,' she added drily.

He met her eyes. 'Amazing,' he murmured, but this time there was no amusement or mockery in the tone; he was totally serious.

Something twisted and turned inside Lauren. It wasn't that she was jealous, she told herself fiercely. She was glad for them both.

The aircraft landed safely on the beach and Cole switched the engines off before turning to speak to her again.

'I'm glad you're here, Lauren,' he said softly. 'And I'm very glad we're friends again.'

Lauren couldn't find her voice to answer that. She didn't know what to say.

Cole searched her face for a moment with dark, intense eyes, then he shrugged lightly and turned away. 'Right, well, let's get moving.' His manner was brisk now as he unfastened his safety-belt, and climbed out to join the members of crew who had walked across to greet them.

Lauren took her time getting out, and her heart sank as she saw Donna walking towards her.

'We didn't think we'd see you out here today, Lauren,' she said by way of a greeting. 'Jon told me you were staying back at the hotel.'

Lauren shrugged. 'Well, I changed my mind. Cole more or less insisted that I come along.'

'Well, he would have, of course. He does tend to worry about you.'

'Worry about me?' Lauren frowned.

'Of course he does.' Donna ran a smoothing hand down over the beautiful swimsuit that was fitted to perfection over her curvaceous figure. 'We don't like to think you might be still upset about us getting together. I hope when we get back to California you will come out to the ranch to visit us, Lauren. I know Cole would like that. It will show that there are no hard feelings; he's still very fond of you.'

'Come on, Donna.' It was Cole's voice calling her impatiently from the other side of the helicopter. 'We're waiting for you.'

'Coming.' With a bright smile at Lauren the other woman turned to walk towards the camera crew.

'Wonderful, isn't she?' Jon came to stand next to her and followed her gaze over towards Donna. 'A stunning-looking girl.'

'Stunning,' Lauren agreed, and then hastily turned her eyes away from the sight of Cole walking with his hand resting on her smooth brown bare back.

'Thought you weren't coming out here today,' Jon said curiously now. 'Couldn't keep away from me, eh?'

'Something like that,' Lauren agreed distantly. She wasn't really listening; she was trying not to think about Donna's words to her, but without much success. That woman always managed to make her feel blazing mad, and that fact made her even more angry. She wanted so much to be emotionally cold to it all. After all, she didn't care.

'Did you ring Warren?' Jon asked curiously now.

'Too early in the day for that. It will have to wait until later. I have confirmed that Cole is giving up his music career; he won't be doing any more tours.'

'You've got that from Adams himself?' Jon asked with rising interest.

'That's a direct quote,' she told him in a businesslike tone. 'So Warren should be pleased with that juicy bit of information.'

'Pleased? He'll be ecstatic.' Jon put an enthusiastic arm around her shoulder and kissed the side of her cheek. 'We've got a major scoop even without the wedding story—it's wonderful.'

'Yes, it is,' Lauren agreed with him, and forced herself to return his smile. She should be feeling pleased: they were getting a good story. Yet for some reason deep down inside she felt everything was far less than wonderful.

As she turned to follow the camera crew further down the beach she caught Cole's gaze. He was watching her with a look on his face that was less than friendly; in fact he looked furiously angry with her.

She frowned and glanced hurriedly away. What had she done to warrant such a look? she wondered nervously.

'I can't wait for this party this evening,' Jon was continuing on now, his arm dropping to circle her waist as they walked. 'This is turning out to be a very pleasurable assignment, don't you think?'

'Well, the weather is a definite bonus,' Lauren said as they came to a standstill under the shade of some palm trees. As far as she was concerned the weather and the beauty of the place were the only pleasurable things about the assignment. The thought of the party this evening was not particularly thrilling.

She glanced over towards Cole again and once more caught that dark expression on his face. It made a shiver of apprehension run right through her. Somehow she had the feeling that the party this evening was going to be nothing short of traumatic.

CHAPTER SEVEN

THE first thing Lauren noticed when she got back to her hotel bedroom late that afternoon was the black silk dress from Amanda's boutique hanging on the outside of her wardrobe.

She went across to it and lifted the plastic covering to gaze once more at the beautiful dress. She ran her hand thoughtfully over the smooth sheen of the material. Obviously Cole had arranged for the dress to be delivered to her room.

She remembered what he had said to her earlier that afternoon about the dress being a present from one friend to another, given with love. Just the memory of those words made her heart skip about in a crazy way. Of course he hadn't meant love as in the way he loved Donna. He had been speaking as a friend.

She turned away from the dress and walked into the bathroom to run a shower. She didn't know what to do about the gift. She felt that she didn't really want Cole as a friend, and she certainly didn't want him feeling sorry for her.

Lauren got undressed and stood under the full-force jet of the shower. The very thought that Cole might pity her made her heart thud angrily. She needed nobody's sympathy; she was a happy, independent woman and she had long since got over Cole Adams.

She stepped out of the shower and towel-dried her body and then her hair with brisk, angry movements. She wouldn't accept the dress. She would send it back down to the boutique.

Her mind made up, she moved back into the bedroom and opened her wardrobe to pick out something to wear for tonight. She had nothing even remotely suitable except her blue dress, and she had worn that last night for dinner.

She closed the doors and looked again at the black dress. Everyone would be very dressed up tonight. She really needed something special and she had been going to buy it anyway. 'Oh, what the heck?' she muttered under her breath, and unzipped the plastic covering.

So it was that some time later she stood in front of the mirror dressed in black silk. It looked stunning on her, the simplicity of style exuding elegance.

She had caught her blonde curls up in diamond clasps that glinted as they caught the overhead lights, leaving her neck and shoulders bare. Her skin was translucent, her eyes large pools of blue.

She remembered the way Cole had looked at her in this dress, the dark gleam in his eyes, then other disturbing memories intruded: the way he had kissed her last night, the softness of his lips against hers.

A light rap on the door interrupted the train of thought and she hurriedly turned to open it, her hands none too steady on the door-handle, her legs strangely shaky.

'Wow, you look fabulous!' Jon's gaze moved from the tip of her toes up over the curves of her body.

She smiled, feeling perfectly at ease with the compliment and the sweeping appraisal. Strange how Cole had studied her appearance in much the same way this afternoon and her reaction had been totally different, his scrutiny sending her into a complete state of turmoil.

'Did you ring Warren?' she asked, forcing her mind away from Cole. They had decided on the way back to the hotel that he should make the call. Or rather, he had decided that he should take some of the praise for getting the story, just in case he didn't get to hang around for the actual wedding.

'Of course I did, and needless to say he was very pleased. All that remains now is to get the pictures of this wedding and I'll be flavour of the year back in that office.'

'Well, we shouldn't have so long to wait,' Lauren said, trying very hard to keep her voice neutral. 'Not now they've finished filming. And Cole paid for the wedding outfits at Amanda's boutique today, so I guess the wedding will be in a few days' time.'

Jon rubbed his hands together in glee. 'This has to be the easiest assignment I've had in a long time.'

And it had to be the toughest she had ever had, Lauren thought as she picked up her handbag and headed with Jon for the door. Emotionally it was tearing her apart inside.

The heavy pulsating rhythm of one of Cole's most popular records greeted them as they stepped through the doors out on to the terrace. Already the party seemed to be in full swing; the terrace was filled with people, some sitting at tables, some dancing on the small, intimate floor that was situated down some steps in the garden. Palm trees had been strung with colourful fairy lights that sparkled like jewels against the darkness of the tropical night. A magnificent buffet had been laid out along the edge of the terrace and chefs looking resplendent in their whites were behind ready to help serve any of the guests who moved along it.

Lauren's eyes moved through the crowd. She recognised quite a few famous faces, and in different circumstances she would have paused to take in exactly who was there, but at the moment she could summon very little enthusiasm. Instead she found herself scanning the crowds looking for Cole's tall figure.

'Lauren, you look fabulous!' Amanda detached herself from a group of people and made a direct line for her.

Lauren smiled at her. 'Thanks, Amanda, so do you.' The other girl did look very beautiful. She was wearing an emerald-green dress that fitted her slim figure perfectly. A matching emerald and diamond necklace at her throat complemented the outfit and the sparkling brightness of her eyes.

'If you're looking for Cole, I think he's down by the pool. We set up another bar down there,' Amanda said with a smile.

Before Lauren had a chance to say that they were not looking for him at all, Jon caught hold of her arm and started to lead her away. 'Thanks, Amanda,' he said with a grin. 'We'll go and find them.'

Lauren didn't want to go and find them at all, but she forced herself to smile and move with him towards the steps. As they walked down towards the pool her eyes moved to the dance-floor. Among the couples dancing she could see Donna and Cole.

For a moment her footsteps faltered and she stopped halfway down the steps, her eyes riveted on the couple. They looked so right together. Donna was wearing a figure-hugging dress in a vivid shade of red. She looked dramatically attractive beside Cole's powerfully dark figure. Her arms were twined up around his neck and as Lauren watched he bent his head and kissed her very softly, very tenderly against her lips.

The feelings that assailed Lauren as she watched them were indescribable; it was as if someone were reaching down inside her very soul and enveloping her heart with cold hands that twisted and turned, tearing her apart with pain.

She swallowed hard and had to fight against a sudden impulse to turn tail and run, run as far away as it was possible to get.

'Lauren?' Jon looked around to see why she had stopped following him and then came back up to stand beside her. 'Anything wrong?' he asked with some concern.

'No, of course not.' She smiled at him brightly, too brightly really, as she forced herself not to give in to the tumultuous feeling raging inside. 'It's just that I've spotted Cole.' She indicated the dance-floor and his eyes moved over the crowds out there and easily located them.

'Wow, Donna looks good,' Jon murmured under his breath. 'They make a very striking couple.'

'I think they're probably ideally suited,' Lauren said matter-of-factly.

Jon glanced at her again and then offered her his hand as they walked down the remainder of the steps. She took it, mainly because the sparkle of lights and the vivid turquoise of the floodlit pool below seemed to have temporarily merged in a hazy shimmer of tears. She angled her head higher and took a firm hold on her wayward emotions. What on earth was the matter with her? she wondered frantically. She knew Cole and Donna were about to be married; why on earth should watching them kiss come as such a shock to her system?

At the bottom of the steps the shadowy hues of the garden started to take shape again as she regained her composure, but she retained her hold on Jon's hand, somehow glad of its reassuring pressure.

'Let's sit down, shall we?' Jon stopped by a quiet table next to the pool. 'I reckon we both deserve a drink.'

'Wonderful idea,' she agreed, forcing a cheerful smile on to her face.

He sat opposite and, leaning across, he once more took hold of her hand in his. 'Have I told you what a pleasure it is to work with you?' he asked with a grin.

'A million or more times.' She had to smile now and this time it was with genuine amusement. Jon never failed to tell her that at the end of every assignment they had been on. He usually followed it with some kind of chat-up line. She never took him seriously because he did have a bit of a reputation back at the paper for being a womaniser, and anyway she didn't find him attractive in that way. To her he was just Jon, a very pleasant colleague.

'You're a terrific lady, do you know that, Lauren?' he said lightly now.

'Of course she knows it.' It was Cole's voice coming from directly behind her, his deep tone slightly mocking.

Lauren could feel her whole body tensing up at his presence. She turned to look at him, trying very hard to look cool and unruffled.

Donna was holding on lightly to his arm and her eyes met Lauren's with a cold, hard look that was openly antagonistic.

Lauren glanced away and straight into Cole's dark eyes. He was watching her closely, and he too looked less than pleased. The expression on his face was the same as the way he had looked at her today down on the beach: it was brooding and intense and she couldn't quite figure it out.

'Would the two of you care to join us?' Jon asked good-naturedly. He released Lauren's hand and pulled out the chair next to him in invitation to Donna.

Lauren cringed inside and hoped they would refuse the invite.

'Thanks.' Cole's tone was dry. He pulled out the chair next to Lauren and sat down, leaving Donna to sit next to Jon.

'Well, what are we having to drink?' Cole enquired crisply as he indicated to one of the waitresses that he wished to place an order.

Out of politeness Lauren had to turn towards him, and she promptly wished that she had done no such thing as her eyes collided with his. He was sitting far too close to her, she thought with rising panic. So close that she could smell the familiar aroma of his cologne. And he looked fantastic, far too attractive for any woman's peace of mind. The dark suit looked superb on his powerful frame, the white silk shirt emphasised the dark mahogany tan of his skin and the jet-black thickness of his hair.

'Well?' he prompted her, and for one crazy second she was reminded of that first day when they had met in that restaurant with Edward Carter. She felt just the way she had felt then, totally out of her depth and breathless with a mixture of nerves and a strange kind of excitement.

'Let's have champagne, darling,' Donna purred from across the table. 'After all, we do have a lot to celebrate. The video is finished and the day after tomorrow is our big day.'

Lauren came quickly down to earth with a bump.

'OK, champagne it is,' Cole agreed easily as he gave the order to the attractive Thai waitress.

Lauren met Jon's eye across the table and he gave her a conspiratorial wink. Obviously he was delighted to get that titbit of knowledge. 'So, the day after tomorrow is the big day, Donna?' he repeated in a probing tone of voice, obviously hoping she would enlighten them further.

'Sure is. Cole and I have our outfits all ready.' Donna's voice was alive with excitement and enthusiasm. 'You should see my dress, Lauren. Amanda has done an incredible job for me.'

'She's a very talented designer.' Lauren desperately tried to summon up some enthusiasm in her tone, but inside there was this flat, dead feeling. The day after tomorrow Cole was getting married.

The champagne arrived and Cole uncorked it with unhurried ease and poured them all a glass of the sparkling liquid into tall long-stemmed glasses placed before them.

'To a successful future,' he said, raising his glass.

'To us,' Donna said softly.

Lauren felt as if the sparkling liquid would choke her; she barely let it touch her lips before she replaced her glass back on the table. She noticed that Cole hardly touched his either.

Across the floodlit pool on the other side of the patio large video screens were automatically rolling down.

'Jed is going to show some of the rushes from today's shoot,' Cole remarked drily with a nod across at them. 'He said he'd get them together in time for a sneak preview of some of the video.'

The music changed tempo to an upbeat rhythm that was moody and strangely haunting, and suddenly Donna was emblazoned over both screens, her body moving sensuously in time with the music.

'Wow!' Jon turned his chair slightly for a better view. 'You look stunning, Donna.'

Stunning was putting it mildly. The other woman had a photogenic quality that captured and held every person at the party. Every head was turned and glued to the screens.

She was wearing a slinky black bikini and walking out of a clear turquoise sea with a backdrop of sharply rising mountains behind her. She had a voice that, although it could never be described as technically brilliant, captured each chord in a way that was uniquely different and catchy. It was the kind of song that could and probably would rise to the top of the charts.

As the last notes melted away into the surging sound of waves pounding against the shore of the deserted beach, there was a unanimous thunderous round of applause from everyone watching.

'You were brilliant.' Jon turned to her and gave her a spontaneous kiss on her cheek. 'Absolutely brilliant. When can I buy the album?'

Donna laughed, and turned questioning eyes on Cole, waiting for his approval. He gave her that slow grin of his that was guaranteed to make any woman's day. 'You were perfect,' he told her gently. 'I told you you would be, a sex symbol in the making.'

Her smile was radiant now, and as the applause grew even more insistent she stood up to receive it with a gracious nod around at everyone.

Jed came down the steps towards them with a wide grin. 'Didn't think I would have that ready so quickly, did you?' he said teasingly to Donna, and put an arm around her shoulders. 'You knocked everyone dead. Cole was right about you.' He grinned over at his boss. 'You always were good at picking a winner.'

'I've got a good eye for spotting talent,' he said with a laugh. 'What did you think of our budding star, Lauren?' He turned abruptly to include her in the conversation. 'Will you give her a good write-up in your article?'

'Yes, I will,' Lauren acknowledged with quiet sincerity. 'You were wonderful.'

For a moment the two women were in a silent world of their own as their eyes met directly. Then Donna turned with a smile towards Cole, stretching out one hand towards him.

'And there is so much in front of us for the future,' she said huskily. 'So much.'

He smiled indulgently at her. 'We've only just started,' he agreed. 'Stick with me, baby; you're going all the way to the top.'

Some more people came over to the table to congratulate Donna and for a while talk revolved solely around her voice and the song and the business of music.

Watching them, Lauren couldn't help thinking how right they were for each other. They could talk on the same level, both of them lived in a world where music was their priority, their love of it and their great talent giving them a bond that she would never have achieved with Cole.

She met Jon's eyes across the table as he smiled ruefully. 'Want to dance?' He mouthed the words silently and she nodded, grateful to escape.

The dance-floor was crowded with couples moving slowly in the warm night air to a romantic ballad. Jon put his arm around her and held her close as they joined the throng of people.

'Ever felt out of place?' he whispered close to her ear.

She tipped her head back and smiled regretfully up at him. 'We are not exactly in with the music jet-set.'

His arm moved closer against the silk of her dress, holding her against his body in a way that was vaguely reassuring. 'How do you feel about this wedding now that it's looming so close?' he asked, resting his cheek against the softness of her hair.

She shrugged and took a deep breath. 'It's an assignment like any other,' she said lightly.

She closed her eyes and all of a sudden for some reason her mind was filled with images of the way Cole had kissed her the other night. It had meant nothing, of course. Cole had been proving a point. Cole had always had an almighty arrogance; finding a woman who had failed to respond to him would have been like a prize fighter suddenly discovering he had lost his right hook.

Now that he knew he could still stir a passionate response in her he could forget her.

But could she forget him? The question burned over and over in her mind. Of course she could, she told herself firmly. Hadn't she done a good job in doing just that over the last few months? Once this assignment was over everything would be back to normal and she could pick up her life in London, maybe start to socialise again. Get herself a boyfriend, someone steady and reliable with a down-to-earth job. The prospect didn't exactly fill her with pleasure for some reason.

She mentally tried to pull herself out of the depressed state she seemed to be lapsing into, and looked up at Jon.

'By all accounts it doesn't look as if we'll be here much longer, not if the wedding is the day after tomorrow. Maybe when we get back to London we could go out for dinner some time?' he asked suddenly.

She smiled. 'Maybe, but it *would* just be dinner, Jon,' she emphasised the fact firmly.

'Spoil-sport.' He dipped his head lower towards her ear. 'I reckon you've still got a soft spot for Adams,' he whispered huskily.

She backed her head away from him and glared at him angrily. 'That's utter rubbish.'

'You think so?' Jon shrugged. 'Well, I disagree. And I'll tell you something further. Wedding or no wedding, I'd say Cole isn't totally immune to you either; in fact I'd say the guy wouldn't mind a little fling before he ties the knot in a couple of days' time.'

Lauren looked up at him, horrified. 'That's an awful thing to say,' she accused him angrily.

'Maybe, but I've never been one to turn my eye away from the truth. Cole is very fond of a pretty woman and he has a certain gleam in his eye when he looks at you that I recognise all too well as lust rearing its fiery head.'

Anger swept through her at such a distasteful statement, but before she had a chance to reprimand him he was dipping his head close to her again and murmuring in an undertone, 'And, speak of the devil, he's coming this way with a very purposeful gleam in his eye.'

The next moment she felt a cool hand against her shoulder, and a huskily dry tone enquiring if he could have the next dance.

'Of course.' Jon stood back from her with a sardonic smile. 'Take good care of her,' he quipped lightly.

Cole glanced down at Lauren, and, seeing her displeasure at that remark, he grinned. 'I'll try my best,' he said drily. 'I'll try my best.' His arms went around her and took her away from Jon in a gently sweeping movement.

She glared up at him, her blue eyes ice-cold; she was still very annoyed with Jon but she felt furious with Cole for some unknown reason. 'Actually, I really don't want to dance to this record,' she told him crisply. 'And I don't care for being passed around like some parcel without being asked properly.'

'Didn't I ask you properly?' One dark eyebrow lifted in amusement. 'My sincere apologies; I thought I had. What would you have liked—for me to go down on one knee?'

Her lips tightened. 'Very droll, Cole. You'll forgive me if I don't find you at all amusing.'

'Of course you do,' he said arrogantly, and his arms slipped down around her waist, pulling her closer. 'You're far too tense these days, Lauren—you seem to have forgotten how to relax.'

Her heart started to pound with a rhythm that was most uncomfortable and she pulled back from him, refusing to allow her body to rest against his. 'That's because I'm not here to relax, I'm here to work,' she told him crisply. 'Why are you so intent on making my work difficult?'

'Am I?' He sounded vaguely amused by her now.

'You know damn well you are,' she muttered under her breath. 'You have refused to let me interview you properly for the details of your wedding and you do nothing but aggravate and torment me.'

'Well, it's never been my policy to make life easy for a reporter.' He sounded very amused now. 'But I must say that I think I've made an exception to that rule for you, both in the past and now.'

She tipped her head back to stare up at him. She wished he wouldn't mention the past; she didn't want to think about it.

'The last time you came to interview me with that fellow Carter, for instance. I went out of my way to——'

'I really don't want to discuss that, Cole,' she cut across him tersely. 'But perhaps, as you are going so much out of your way to co-operate with me, you would like to tell me when you're leaving this hotel? Do you intend to get married here?'

Dark eyes swept over her sardonically. 'I intend to leave here after I've tied up a few loose ends tomorrow. Maybe around lunchtime. Will that suit you?'

'Now you're being facetious,' she told him angrily. She knew very well that he didn't care a damn what suited her.

'You're very determined to stay angry with me, aren't you, Lauren?' His voice had a dangerously soft edge. 'Have you stopped to consider why, I wonder?'

'I don't have to stop to consider that question. The answer is pretty damn obvious. You infuriate me.'

'You mean I stir up feelings you don't want to acknowledge.' He stroked the silky skin at the side of her neck with the edge of his thumb. Then he leaned closer to whisper against her ear, 'That's a little closer to the truth, isn't it?'

'What do you want me to say to that, Cole?' she demanded icily. 'That I find you irresistible? Is that ego of yours really so great that you want to know that every woman is pining away for you?'

'Yes,' he agreed with her in a teasing amused tone. 'A certain PR girl once wrote that no woman could resist my charms. I'm just testing out if she knew what she was talking about.'

Lauren's cheeks flared with colour; she remembered very clearly writing that line. 'I never thought you were the type of man to believe your own publicity, Cole.'

'You mean that the stuff that you wrote about me was all fabrication?' He sounded as if he was finding this all highly entertaining. 'Well, this is a severe blow.' He moved closer, holding her body firmly against his. 'Surely there was some truth in your words? How about the line you used to murmur in my ear as we made love?'

She moved furiously against him, trying with all her strength to move away. Her heart was beating so loudly that it seemed to fill her head with its insistent hammering. He wouldn't allow her to break away from him. He held her with frightening ease against his chest. 'How did that line go, Laurie?' he asked in a low, deep tone.

'Stop it, Cole.' She shook her head, refusing to allow her brain to travel down the dangerous path of remembrance he was so intent on leading her down.

'How did it go, Laurie?' He murmured the words in a husky tone next to her ear. 'I love you, Cole... wasn't that what you used to whisper?'

She twisted her head away from him. How could he talk so mockingly of such intense private moments? She took a deep steadying breath, willing herself to gain control of the emotions teeming inside her.

'Lauren?' His hand moved upwards to stroke the side of her hair and she flinched from the caress.

'Don't.' When she finally found her voice it sounded breathless and unsteady. 'Don't make fun of me in this way. I won't stand for it.'

'I'm not making fun, Lauren.' His hands moved to cup her head, turning her to face him, forcing her to look up into his dark eyes.

'No?' Her eyes glimmered brightly blue. 'What do you call it when you tease me about... about such an intimate moment... about things that are best forgotten?'

'I call it facing up to the truth,' he answered steadily. 'Something you seem afraid of. The fact is that we can deny it all we like but we are still attracted to each other—there is still a physical pull that draws us together whether we like it or not——'

'No, that's just not true.' She shook her head vehemently. 'If we are going to face up to the truth, how about you facing up to the fact that you are about to become a married man? Don't you think it's time you started acting more responsibly instead of making passes at every woman who catches your eye?'

He smiled at that. 'Lauren, I'm not making passes at every woman. Just one very beautiful one in a black Thai silk dress.' His hand moved down over the softness of the material. 'I know I apologised for kissing you the other day, but to be honest that kiss felt so right, it couldn't have been wrong.'

'And what about Donna?' Her voice held a raw bitterness as she fought to get back into the realms of reality. Cole was just playing with her and it was wrong, very wrong both to Donna and to her.

'Donna has nothing to do with us,' he answered evenly.

She glared at him. 'So you don't care about hurting her?'

His lips twisted in a half-smile. 'I won't be hurting Donna, take my word for it—we haven't got that kind of a relationship.'

She stared at him. Was he telling her that his marriage to Donna was going to be open? That they both intended to indulge in affairs? The mere thought of it was distasteful to Lauren. Anger lent her body strength as she pulled away from him. 'I really don't care what kind of a relationship you have with Donna; just keep me out of it. I have no wish to be involved in your sordid liaisons.'

Before he could make any reply to that she had whirled around and was leaving the dance-floor. Anger was vying with a well of tears deep inside her. Cole's behaviour was intolerable.

Her eyes swept around the crowds of people, anxiously searching for Jon. Tears were shimmering in her eyes, she felt so hurt by Cole's cavalier attitude. The whole evening was just a nightmare. Relief swept through her as she spotted her colleague making his way through the crowds towards the dance-floor. Her relief was short-lived when she saw that he had a tight hold on Donna's hand and was leading her out for a dance.

'Looks as if you've lost your boyfriend for a while.' Cole's droll voice behind her was just the last straw.

'They're just having a dance, for heaven's sake.' She swung around towards him, fury mixing with the mist of tears in her eyes.

One eyebrow lifted and all amusement seemed to fade from the darkly tanned face as he looked down at her. 'If it's just a dance, why are you looking so upset?'

'I'm not upset.' Her chin angled upwards.

'Yes, you are. You know your boyfriend is the type to chase anything in a skirt and you're worried to death.'

'Don't be ridiculous,' she snapped furiously.

'Am I?' He shrugged. 'I've noticed the way he looks at her.'

'Funny, Jon has just said the same about the way you look at me.'

'Did he, now?' Cole murmured contemplatively. 'Not as unperceptive as I thought.'

'Perhaps it just takes one womaniser to recognise another,' Lauren said succinctly. 'Does it bother you that Jon finds your intended bride attractive?' She angled her chin upwards and forced herself to meet his eyes.

There was silence for a moment. Then he said quietly, 'It bothers me more than you will ever know.'

There was such depth of feeling in his voice that for a moment Lauren was taken aback. So much for his open relationship, she thought wryly. It was probably all right for him to stray but not for Donna. It was strange how much it hurt hearing him voicing such intense feeling for the other woman.

'What about you, Lauren? How deep are your feelings for Jon? Does it bother you that he finds Donna attractive?'

She shrugged, not at all at ease with the question. It didn't bother her in the slightest, but she could hardly say that, not after deliberately misleading him about their relationship.

'What if I was to tell you that right at this moment Jon is kissing her?' he asked drily, his eyes moving over Lauren's shoulder towards the dance-floor.

'I'd say you have a perverted sense of humour,' Lauren said with a wry twist of her lips.

'Really?' He put one hand on her shoulder and turned her just in time to see Jon's head nestling in against the side of Donna's face.

For a moment a start of surprise ran through her and then she just shrugged. 'I wouldn't read too much into that, Cole; it won't be what it seems.'

Cole's lips twisted scornfully. 'How understanding you are where Jon is concerned, and how naïve. We'll just say he was giving her mouth-to-mouth resuscitation, then, shall we?' Dark eyes blazed down at her, his mouth was set in a grim line.

As she glanced up at the powerfully attractive features it struck her suddenly that Cole was jealous.

It hurt to know he was so possessive of Donna, and her hands clenched into tight fists at her side. This whole situation was getting to her; she didn't know just how much more her raw emotions could take. She felt like crying again, and that just wasn't like her.

'Lauren?' Cole's voice broke into her thoughts and it sounded gently concerned now. The dark eyes that moved over her pale features held a gentle light now as he noted her distress. 'I'm sorry, sweetheart, I probably shouldn't have drawn your attention to Jon.'

She shrugged. 'I don't care, Cole, really I don't.' Her voice cracked and the tremulous emotions that were flowing through her showed all too clearly for a moment, telling him just how much she did care; but it wasn't for Jon, it was for him.

Her eyes moved hungrily over the dark features. She still loved him, the realisation hit her forcibly out of nowhere.

'He's certainly not worth your tears,' Cole murmured softly, and he lifted a hand and stroked softly over her cheek. She was horrified to find it was damp with tears and she stepped back and away from him.

'I'm not upset, Cole, I'm just feeling a little over-tired.' She angled her chin up defiantly.

'No, of course you're not upset,' he murmured sardonically. He reached out a hand to catch hold of her arm. 'Don't cry, Lauren,' he said softly.

'I'm not; I've told you I'm not.' She shrugged off his hand and moved away from him. She had to get out of here before she broke down and made a complete fool of herself. 'If you'll excuse me I think I'll go and look for Amanda.' Without giving him a chance to say anything to that, she moved away through the crowds. But she wasn't looking for Amanda; she was looking for the sanctuary of her own room. She just wanted to cry and cry. Her whole world felt as if it had just collapsed around her. She was still in love with Cole and the day after next he would be marrying Donna.

CHAPTER EIGHT

HER room was cool after the tropical heat of the night, yet Lauren felt as if she was burning up. She made her way into the bathroom and splashed her face with cold water.

How could she still be in love with Cole? she asked herself furiously. After the way he had hurt her in the past, and especially now when he was about to marry another woman. Had she no sense, no self-respect? She stared at her reflection in the bathroom mirror, at the pale skin and wide, haunted eyes, then turned away from herself in disgust.

The sound of the bedroom door opening sent her hurrying back into the other room. She came to an abrupt halt at the sight of Cole standing just inside.

'What do you want?' Her voice trembled slightly. 'And don't you think you should knock before barging into my bedroom?'

His mouth curved in a half-smile. 'I hardly think I'm going to see anything that I haven't seen before.'

White-hot anger gripped her. He was so arrogant, so sure of himself.

'How are you feeling?' he asked drily.

'I feel fine; there's nothing wrong with me.' She lifted her chin defiantly, and at the same time she wondered if her face was still streaked with tears.

'That's why you're hiding alone in your bedroom, is it?' he asked lazily. 'You didn't find Amanda, I take it?'

She shook her head. 'I decided I felt tired. I just want to be left alone, Cole.'

'I don't think that's a good idea, not while you're so upset.' He took a step towards her and she backed away.

'Please go away.' There was a pleading note in her voice that he couldn't have failed to hear, yet he continued to walk towards her with arrogant slowness, a gleam of purpose in his dark eyes.

'Please, Cole.' She was in complete panic as he came closer. If he touched her she didn't know what she might do. She was keeping a brave face by just the finest thread of control.

She backed up against the bedside table. 'Get out of here before I throw something at you.'

One dark eyebrow lifted mockingly. 'Go ahead,' he invited lazily.

Her fingers reached compulsively for the first thing that came to hand. 'I'm warning you, just leave.' There was a threatening note in her voice now as she lifted a heavy vase.

'I hope for your sake that you're not planning to throw that,' he said in a perfectly calm voice, yet there was a note of caution there that nobody in their right mind would have ignored.

'I just might.' She remained defiant against all her other instincts. She didn't want to throw the beautiful vase and she didn't know if she was brave enough to face Cole's anger, yet she knew that she couldn't let him anywhere near her. To do so was inviting disaster in her present frame of mind.

He stood in front of her and reached out calmly for the vase.

'Please, Cole.' Her voice was a mere whisper in the silence of the room. It was filled with distress, filled with an overwhelming panic.

He simply ignored her and reached out to take the vase from suddenly nerveless fingers to place it back where it belonged.

'That's better.' His eyes never left the paleness of her face. 'Now, shall we talk about it?'

'About what?' She licked suddenly dry lips.

He reached out a hand and gently stroked a stray curl from her forehead. 'About the look on your face when you saw Jon and Donna together.' His hand moved to rest at the side of her neck. 'I know it hurts you, Lauren, but believe me, Jon isn't worth you getting so upset. You're vulnerable and——'

'For goodness' sake, Cole!' She tried to brush his hand away impatiently. 'You're starting to sound like an agony aunt. You know nothing about how I feel.'

'I know that I don't like to see you so upset.' He caught her hand in his and the next moment she was being pulled in close against him.

For a moment she allowed herself to lean against him. It was heaven being held like this. The broad chest, the strong lines of his body were so familiar to her. She closed her eyes and allowed herself to savour the moment. She breathed in the fresh scent of his cologne and remembered how good it had once been between them. This man was so dear to her, no one would ever be able to take his place.

'Cole.' She leaned back to look up at him. Then, as her eyes met his, she forgot completely what she was going to say. 'Cole.' Her arms sneaked up the smooth material of his dark suit to wind their way around his neck. Then she was standing on tiptoe to press her lips against his.

For just a second he didn't respond and she increased the pressure of her lips. Then he met her kisses with a hungry urgency that took her breath away. His lips swept her away on a tide of desire; all that mattered was being in his arms.

His hand curved around her slender waist and lingered on the silk-covered buttons there.

'Lauren?' His eyes were dark with desire as he stared down at her.

She knew what he was asking her and her answer was an unequivocal yes as she pressed her body closer to his. She didn't want to think about the rights and wrongs of their being together tonight; all she knew was that she needed him, that she wanted him with all her heart.

The black dress rustled as the buttons were easily unfastened and the dress slithered over slim hips in a silky fluid wave to land with a whisper on the carpet.

His lips left hers to blaze a heated trail down the side of her neck. His hands moved to her hair and it tumbled from the diamond clasps in a glossy curtain of blonde curls.

The jacket of the suit joined the silk at their feet and then he was lifting her towards the bed. For a moment he paused, his eyes moving over the slender curves of her body clad only in scanty lace underwear. 'You're so beautiful, Laurie,' he whispered huskily. 'And right at this moment I've never wanted anyone as much as I want you.'

She smiled tremulously and her hands swept gently up the white silk of his shirt to unfasten his tie. Then slender fingers started to unbutton his shirt.

He placed one strong hand over hers, halting her momentarily, and her eyes flew to lock with his dark gaze.

'We need to talk before we go any further,' he told her gently.

Dark lashes hid the brilliant blue of her eyes for a moment as she shook her head. 'I don't want to talk, Cole. I just want you to make love to me.' She didn't want to hear him point out that this was just a one-night affair, that he was still going to marry Donna. She wanted to blank those thoughts out with the pleasure of being held in his arms.

'Laurie——' She cut his words off with the softness of her lips. Anything else he had to say to her was lost in the heat of passion.

Strands of light were reaching out across the bedroom floor when Lauren surfaced momentarily from the hazy mists of sleep. She was entwined closely next to Cole, his arm holding her protectively in against his chest. She snuggled even closer and he opened his eyes.

'I wondered when you were going to wake up.' He smiled down at her and kissed the top of her head. 'I was wrestling with my conscience as to whether I should disturb you, and I'm afraid my more basic instincts were winning.'

'And what basic instincts are those?' She smiled shyly up at him and then laughed as he swept her around so that she was firmly pinned beneath him.

'These, of course.' His lips found hers in a crushing kiss filled with desire.

It was a while before the insistent ring of the telephone penetrated through to Lauren's conscious mind. 'Cole.'

'Mmm?' He raised his head briefly to look at her.

'The phone.' Her voice was a mere whisper as she reluctantly drew his attention to the interruption.

'It might look better if you answer it.' He pulled away from her and smiled down at her ruefully. 'We don't want to ruin your reputation.'

Cold reality crept slowly into Lauren's heart as she forced herself to sit up. Of course, he wouldn't want Donna to know that he was here with her.

She raked a trembling hand through her tousled blonde curls, pulling them back from her face as she reached for the receiver.

'Lauren?' There was no mistaking Donna's cool, crisp tones. 'Have you seen Cole?'

Before Lauren could formulate a reply the other woman went on tearfully, 'No one has seen him since the party last night, and we have a crisis on our hands. There was an accident with the final rushes of the video last night and Jed thinks we might have to shoot a few scenes again.'

Lauren frowned. 'What happened?'

'I don't know... they fell in the swimming-pool or something,' Donna muttered offhandedly. 'If you see him tell him I'm looking for him.' The phone was slammed down.

Lauren replaced the receiver and turned her attention towards Cole. 'Did you hear that?'

'Certainly did.' Cole's face was grim as he swung his legs out of the bed. 'Sorry, sweetheart, but it looks as if I'd better go and sort this out.'

Lauren watched him getting dressed. Her heart felt as if someone was squeezing it with cold, clammy hands. Cole was running back to Donna, back to his work, the two most important things in his life. Last night had just been a pleasant distraction, something that had already been forgotten.

Guilt flooded through her. How could she have allowed him to make love to her last night? She had more or less flung herself at a man who was about to be married to another woman. What kind of a person was she to have allowed such a thing to happen?

He finished buttoning up his shirt and leaned across to kiss her. 'We might have to delay leaving today.'

She nodded; somehow she just couldn't find her voice. Guilt was mingling with her overwhelming love for this man and it was tearing her apart.

'How about having lunch with me?' He was being kind now, behaving in a civilised manner about the whole affair.

Again she just nodded.

He frowned, the handsome features drawn for a moment. Then he glanced at his watch. 'OK, see you about one and we'll talk.' He kissed her cheek and stood up from the bed. He turned briefly before opening the door. He looked lazily attractive, his dark hair slightly dishevelled, his jacket slung casually over the white silk shirt. 'By the way...' The strong mouth curved in a lop-sided grin. 'Thanks for last night, Lauren; it was very special.'

Then the door closed behind him and he was gone. Lauren sank down into the softness of the bed and stared dry-eyed up at the ceiling. Last night had been wrong—Cole wasn't hers; he belonged to Donna. Yet she loved him—she loved him so much it was like an actual pain burning deep inside her heart.

She glanced at her watch. It was just after seven in the morning. She wondered how she was going to get through the day, how was she going to look Donna in the eye. Would Cole be truthful about where he'd spent last night? Would Donna be very hurt if he was? She knew that if she was in the other woman's shoes she would be incredibly hurt. She rolled on her side and buried her face into the pillows. She felt incredibly sad and extremely guilty just knowing that Cole was with her now. This situation was intolerable.

With a sigh she got up and went to have a shower. She wouldn't think about things; she would just take each day as it came. And what about Cole's wedding? a little voice whispered inside. Would she be able to cover it and write her story with an unbiased ease? A shudder ran through her at the very thought.

A little while later, dressed in a pale blue dress, she made her way slowly down towards the restaurant. She bumped into Amanda in the foyer and the girl stopped her with a bright smile.

'How are you this morning, Lauren?'

'Fine, how are you?'

The girl rolled her eyes heavenwards. 'A little bit of a headache, but I don't think I'm the only one. Jon is in the restaurant looking very sorry for himself. Too much Mekhong last night.' Amanda grinned. 'It was quite a good party, though, wasn't it? It went on until four this morning, you know—were you still there to see Donna's party piece?'

'The video? Yes, she was very good. I think Cole is right, she will be a big star,' Lauren agreed.

Amanda shook her head. 'No, not the video, although that was very good. I'm talking about her making a complete spectacle of herself by tossing some of the team's video equipment into the swimming-pool. Part of the video was ruined, apparently.'

Lauren frowned. 'Donna threw their video in the pool?'

'Well, part of it. She was quite drunk at the time, ranting on about Cole cheating on her. Jed had to lift her up bodily and take her to her room.'

Lauren's face burnt with guilty colour. So Donna had known that Cole had come after her and stayed in her room.

'Lord alone knows what Cole will say when he finds out,' Amanda continued. 'He had disappeared off somewhere and no one could find him.'

Lauren cringed and tried to change the subject quickly. 'Maybe we won't be leaving today after all.'

Amanda shrugged. 'I don't know. We have a recording studio up on the top floor. A lot of our guests are in the music business, so it's handy for them if they want to do a little work. Cole's up there in the offices sorting things out. You could nip up and see what's going on if you want; I'm sure Cole wouldn't mind.'

But Donna would, Lauren thought wretchedly. 'I'll go up after I've had some breakfast,' she murmured.

The very thought of looking into Cole's eyes and trying to act as if nothing had happened last night made her heart pump with distress. She couldn't deal with this situation; she wasn't cool and sophisticated enough to act as if she didn't care. She did care—she was in love with the man.

Lauren moved through into the restaurant to find Jon, her mind in turmoil. She just didn't know where to go from here.

Jon was sitting on his own at the far end of the room and she made her way across to him.

'Good morning.' She forced herself to sound cheerful as she took the seat opposite.

'Good morning, and keep your voice down,' Jon grumbled.

Lauren had to laugh. 'Feeling delicate this morning?'

'Something like that.' He reached and poured himself another cup of coffee. 'Did you enjoy the party last night?'

'It was all right. I noticed that you seemed to have enjoyed yourself.'

He looked up at the pointed note in her voice.

'I told you to keep an eye on Donna, Jon, not make a pass at her,' she went on in a light tone.

'I wasn't really making a pass at her, Lauren——' He broke off and grimaced. 'Well, maybe I was,' he admitted in a lower tone. 'Do you think anybody noticed?'

'By anybody I presume you mean Cole, and yes, he did notice. You were wrapped around his fiancée on the dance-floor—of course he noticed!'

'Hell!' Jon raked an unsteady hand through his hair. 'I bumped into Adams this morning; no wonder he looked as if he wanted to thrash me.'

'Yes, no wonder,' Lauren echoed drily.

'Sorry, Lauren,' he murmured. 'I guess I had too much to drink, and she is very attractive.'

'You don't have to apologise to me,' she said with a sigh.

'Well, I'm certainly not going to apologise to Adams,' he muttered, finishing his coffee and pouring them both out a cup from a fresh pot a waiter put down on the table. 'Anyway, he doesn't have to worry about me. I'm not what you would call real competition, not against a man like him.' His voice grated angrily, 'She's totally infatuated with him. Went crazy when both you and Cole went missing from the party.' He gave a raw laugh. 'She threw some of the video equipment into the pool.'

'So I heard,' Lauren murmured.

'So what's the inside story, Lauren?' He looked over at her with enquiring eyes. 'What happened between you and Cole last night?'

'Nothing.' She glanced away from him uncomfortably.

'That's why I bumped into him leaving your room this morning, is it?'

Lauren's face flared a bright crimson red and he held up his hands. 'Sorry. I'm just concerned about you. He's going to marry Donna within a matter of days, and I don't think you should lose sight of that fact.'

'I haven't.' Lauren swallowed hard on the tears that started to gather in her throat.

He nodded. 'But don't mind me, Lauren; I suppose I'm a little jealous.'

'Rubbish,' Lauren said lightly.

He shrugged. 'I know I ended up dancing with Donna last night, but if I'd been given a choice I would have been with you. Personally I think Adams has got the wrong woman.'

'Well, it's nice of you to say that——'

'I'm not being nice,' he cut across her. 'I'm being truthful.' He put his cup down and smiled across at her. 'If you've had enough coffee, I suggest we go back up to your room and get started on this article we need to send to Warren. He'll be expecting something by the end of the week,' Jon briskly brought the conversation around to work, and she nodded gratefully.

Hours later they were still sitting at the desk in Lauren's room trying to agree on what had been written so far.

'This is no good, Lauren,' Jon grated harshly. 'We need to get the two of them together and ask them some direct questions. Half of this is just surmising.' He raked an impatient hand through his hair. 'We still have no idea where they plan to get married. Any time I ask the man a question he dodges it. Sometimes I wonder why the hell he invited us out here; he certainly doesn't seem to want to give us an interview.'

'He always has been reluctant to talk about himself to the Press,' Lauren murmured.

'Yes, but if he's so reluctant to talk to us, why did he invite us out?'

'Your guess is as good as mine.' She shrugged. 'I would think it's because he imagines I won't delve into too many personal details and I won't write anything that will show them in a less than glowing light.' Her voice held a slightly bitter edge as she thought about it.

Jon shook his head. 'I don't know, Lauren; it doesn't sound——' The ringing of the telephone interrupted them and he marched across to lift it impatiently. 'Yes?'

One eyebrow lifted and he placed a hand over the receiver as he turned to Lauren. 'It's Adams for you.'

A tingle of anticipation shot through her as she nodded and went over to take the phone from him with shaking fingers.

'Lauren?' Cole's voice was crisp and authoritative.

'Yes.' She had to fight down the wave of emotion at just hearing that tone. It was a million light-years away from the passion they had shared last night.

'I'm sorry, honey, but we'll have to skip our lunch appointment today.' Despite the endearment his manner was brisk, almost businesslike. 'I don't know how much you know, but apparently Donna had too much to drink last night and the result was that part of the video has been completely wrecked.'

'So I heard.' Lauren tried very carefully to keep her voice as steady as his. 'Is it a serious set-back?'

'Nothing I can't fix,' he said with a grim note of determination. 'I have another copy but it needs editing, so I'll just have to give it my full attention.'

'OK, I understand.' The video was important, more important than a mere lunch date. Lauren was a career girl; she could understand that. Anyway, what could they have said to each other over lunch? She knew that last night hadn't meant as much to him as it had to her. It had been a pleasurable interlude for him; he had probably been angry with Donna and if she was honest with herself she had practically thrown herself at him. Remorse ate away at her at the very thought.

'All right, I'll be in touch later.'

The casual line made her heart ache. 'Fine, see you later.'

She replaced the phone gently, feeling the prick of hot tears behind her eyes. She swallowed hard and tried very hard to compose herself before turning towards Jon. 'They don't have to reshoot the video. Cole had another copy, so it looks as if things aren't so bad after all.'

'Well, that's a relief.' Jon let his breath out in a long whistle. 'For a while there I thought we might be hanging around for quite some time waiting for this wedding.'

'Somehow I don't think we'll be waiting too much longer,' said Lauren in a low tone. She turned away from him and made a pretence of opening up her handbag to get her lipstick out. She didn't care, she told herself crossly. She didn't care.

She moved towards the mirror and carefully applied the pale pink colour to her lips. It brightened her face a little, took the attention away from the haunted shadows in her deep blue eyes. 'Looks as if I've been stood up for lunch.' She forced a smile to those lips as she turned back to him. 'So how about you joining me?'

'Sounds good to me.' Jon straightened the papers in front of him on the desk. 'We can continue with this afterwards and try to get it in to Warren by tomorrow. That should keep him happy for a while.'

Lauren nodded and picked up her bag. Strangely enough, she didn't really care any more about keeping Warren happy. She wished with all her heart that she had never taken this assignment.

The restaurant was practically empty. They took a table in the pretty conservatory part at the far end. It looked out over the glorious colourful gardens towards the white beach and the turquoise of the sea. A heavenly setting and very romantic. Gazing out at it, Lauren allowed herself to daydream for just a moment that last night might have meant something to Cole. He had held her so tenderly, as if he had really cared about her, as if he was glad to have her back in his arms.

'Lauren?' Jon's voice brought her attention back to the table for a moment. He handed her the menu and she opened it and stared down at lists, the words all a hazy blur. Her mind was totally wrapped up in memories of the night before.

Her eyes wandered towards the windows again, thoughts of Cole sweeping through her—how he had whispered her name in the silence of the night, how gentle he had been with her. Surely there had been some deep feelings in those magical moments?

'Isn't that Cole and Donna?' Jon asked, his eyes following hers towards the view outside.

Her eyes moved over the gardens towards the couple he had indicated. They were silhouetted against the blue of the sea. The curve of the man's dark head was achingly familiar and with a jolt she realised it was Cole. Cole with his arms entwined around Donna.

The tentative dreams shattered in one awful crumbling blow as she watched them. Donna was clinging to his broad-shouldered frame, her face tipped back in a provocative way.

'Well, we can relax, I'd say,' Jon said in a voice that was slightly lacking in enthusiasm. 'Looks very much as if the wedding plans are on course.'

'Looks like it.' Lauren turned her head sharply back to the table. Her body was trembling. She felt slightly sick. The floral arrangement of orchids on the table, which had smelt so sweet and beautiful before, was now actually making her feel nauseous.

'You all right?' Jon was staring at her strangely.

'Fine.' She lifted the menu. She wasn't going to cry; she knew the score with Cole and Donna. She had known it last night; it was her own fault that she had allowed her thoughts to turn to fantasy for a short while.

The waiter arrived for their order and Lauren forced herself to pick something from the list in front of her.

When she had left Cole in California she had thought she would never experience such pain and hurt again, and here it was welling up in an unbearable wave inside her once more. Would she never learn her lesson where that man was concerned?

'I think I'll have the tiger prawns,' Jon told the waiter, and then as he left he leaned across to refill Lauren's glass. 'Cheer up, sweetheart,' he said gently. 'We shouldn't be here much longer.'

She shook her head and then suddenly something inside her just cracked. 'Well, I won't be here much longer anyway. I think you should stay, though.'

Jon frowned. 'What are you saying?'

'I'm saying that as soon as I can get a flight out of here I'm going back to London.' She lifted her chin determinedly. Suddenly, now that she had come to a decision, she felt much better.

Jon frowned. 'But you can't! Warren will go mad...we haven't got our story yet.'

Lauren shook her head. 'Right at this moment I couldn't care less about Warren or the newspaper, or for that matter my job. I have to go, Jon.' Her voice broke for a moment on a husky whisper before she continued staunchly, 'Warren has got one scoop about Cole's decision to quit singing. That will have to suffice from me. You can cover the rest.'

Jon shook his head. 'You don't know what you're saying, Lauren. I can't stay on here without you——'

'Yes, you can.' The blue eyes defied him to argue with her. 'After lunch I'm phoning the airport. I have no intention of hanging around here any longer.'

CHAPTER NINE

'LAUREN, you can't do this. Just think about it for a minute. You stand to lose your job. Warren will hit the roof.' Jon was pacing up and down her bedroom floor, looking extremely agitated.

Lauren on the other hand was perfectly cool. Once she had made up her mind she had felt better. It was as if a weight had been lifted off her shoulders. She wouldn't have to stay and witness Cole's wedding; she wouldn't have to hear him make all the promises she had hoped he would one day make to her. She could never have handled that situation.

'It's a risk I'm prepared to take,' she answered calmly.

Jon shook his head in bewilderment. All through lunch he had been trying to get her to change her mind, but it had been like talking to a brick wall. 'I just don't understand you,' he muttered now, flinging himself down on to her bed and glaring up at her. 'You're throwing away the opportunity of a lifetime. Any other reporter would give their right arm to get the inside scoop on Cole's wedding.'

'Perhaps I'm not as dedicated to my career as I like to think,' Lauren answered with a shrug.

'Or perhaps you're letting your heart dictate to you,' he said grimly. 'I think you're still in love with Cole Adams.'

She stared over at him for a moment, then dropped her eyes from his steady gaze. 'Yes, I am,' she whispered the acknowledgement in a low tone. Jon at least deserved to be told the truth; after all, she was letting him down rather badly.

'Oh, Lauren,' he groaned. 'This is because of last night, isn't it? You hoped that there was a chance of the two of you getting back together.'

'I think in my heart I've always known that wasn't possible, but seeing Cole and Donna together today brought it home just how much I cared. It also taught me very sharply just how much it hurt.' She sat down in the chair opposite. 'I'm sorry to let you down, Jon, but I just couldn't hang around for their wedding; it would kill me.'

'I'd like to kill him,' Jon muttered angrily. 'In fact I've got a good mind to go down there now and——'

'No, you can't do that,' she cut across him sharply. 'This is my problem and you won't help it by doing that. The best thing you can do is hang around here and get the story for Warren. That, combined with the story we've already got together on Cole's decision to quit his singing, might pacify him. Maybe then he won't fire me.'

'I wouldn't count on it,' Jon said drily.

Lauren shrugged her slim shoulders and reached for the phone. 'Well, like it or not, I'm going to try and arrange a flight back to England. Besides, I don't think Donna will want me around here, and I can't say I blame her.'

Organising an air ticket turned out to be harder than she had thought. All the flights for the following day were busy. The only thing they could offer her was a flight to Bangkok this evening, then a flight to England the day after next, which meant she would have to stay two nights in a hotel in Bangkok. She only hesitated a moment before accepting that flight. At least she would not have to spend another night in this hotel.

Jon shook his head as she put down the phone. 'I think you're making a big mistake.'

'It would be a worse mistake to stay around here.' Lauren smiled sadly at him. 'Come on, Jon, could you honestly stand by and watch the person you love marry someone else?'

Jon was silent for a moment, then he got up to give her a hug. 'Sorry, Lauren,' he said gruffly. 'I guess I'm not being very sensitive.' He straightened and then grinned. 'Want any help with your packing?'

'Don't go overboard,' she said with a smile. 'But how about us finishing that article before I leave?'

'Sounds like a sensible idea.'

It was late afternoon before they finally finished work. Lauren felt tired, but at least keeping so busy had taken her mind off leaving Cole. Now, as she sat back in her chair and watched Jon tidy away the pile of paper from the desk into his case, she suddenly felt an overwhelming sadness. Once she had left here she would probably never see Cole again.

Jon glanced over at her and caught the expression on her face. 'Are you going to say goodbye to him?' he asked gently.

She shook her head. 'I hate saying goodbye.'

'I think you should. Sometimes it helps to finish things properly, make a clean break, and then you can start afresh at least knowing that there's no animosity between you.'

'I don't know...' Lauren hesitated. 'I'll pack my bags and see about organising a taxi to the airport, then I'll think about it.' She glanced at her watch. 'My flight isn't until seven this evening, so I have plenty of time.'

'OK, it's up to you, anyway.' He frowned as a sudden thought struck him. 'What are you doing about a hotel in Bangkok?'

'I'll just get a taxi to the Sheldon. If they don't have room I'll get the driver to take me to another hotel. Don't worry, Jon, I'm perfectly capable of sorting everything out.'

Her confidence had started to diminish a little by the time she had packed her bags and had a shower. Was she doing the right thing by running away like this? a little voice whispered insistently inside her. And as for saying goodbye to Cole, her heart seemed to freeze at the very thought.

Dressed in a lightweight cotton suit and turquoise suntop, she made her way down to Reception to order a taxi. Once the girl behind the desk had seen to that for her, she asked her tentatively if she knew where Cole Adams could be found.

'Hold on one second.' The girl smiled at her. 'I'll see if I can reach him in his suite.'

Lauren waited patiently for a few moments while the girl phoned through.

'I'm sorry.' The receptionist smiled apologetically as she replaced the receiver. 'I'm afraid there's no answer. He might be still up in the recording studio; should I have him paged?'

Lauren shook her head. 'No, it's all right, I'll go up myself.'

Decisively she made her way to the lifts and stepped in. Jon was right, she decided; she would see Cole and speak to him civilly before she left.

The recording studios occupied most of the top floor. There were numerous offices off them, all filled with the latest high-tech equipment. Lauren was about to give up the idea of finding Cole when a door at the far end of the corridor opened and Jed came out.

'Hello.' He smiled brightly at her. 'I'm just on my way down to the restaurant for dinner. Care to join me?'

She shook her head regretfully. 'Sorry, Jed, I don't really have time.' She nodded her head back in the direction of the room he had just come out of. 'Is Cole up here?'

Jed nodded. 'He's been up here nearly all day. Hopefully he should have the video sorted by this evening.'

'Can I go in and speak to him?'

Jed nodded. 'He's not in too bad a mood, considering what Donna did. I would have thought he would go completely mad with her, but apart from tearing a strip off her this morning he's been remarkably calm. Probably because we had a spare copy of the tape.'

Or because he loved Donna too much to get very angry with her, Lauren thought miserably.

She left Jed and moved to knock on the door. At the sound of Cole's clipped voice asking her to come in she took a deep breath and stepped inside.

Cole wasn't alone—there was another one of his music technicians with him and they were having a heated discussion about a scene that apparently had been cut from the original video.

'Lauren!' Cole turned and saw her. He smiled and his eyes moved lazily over her slender body to linger on the soft cloud of blonde hair that surrounded the pale, delicate face. 'This is a nice surprise.'

He turned to the other man. 'Let's take a ten-minute break on this, shall we?'

The man grinned. 'Whatever you say, boss.' He moved to leave them alone. 'I'll go and get myself some coffee.'

'Get some sent up for us while you're about it.' Cole pulled out one of the chairs for Lauren to sit down at the desk. 'We'll take a coffee-break together,' he said, sitting down beside her.

There was silence for a moment as the door closed, leaving them alone. Cole's gaze held hers, and there was a dark intensity in the black deep pools of his eyes.

'I'm sorry about lunch,' he said gently.

'That's all right; I understand.' Her voice held a husky quality. She wanted so much for him to hold her in his arms. The need was like a physical ache deep inside her.

As always, he looked so incredibly handsome. He was casually dressed in a white shirt that seemed to emphasise the wide, powerful shoulders and a pair of faded blue jeans that hugged his slim hips and long legs. She swallowed hard and looked away from him. This was even more difficult than she had imagined. How could she say goodbye to him without breaking down and making a complete fool of herself?

'I'm glad you came up, Lauren.' He gently stroked a stray strand of her blonde hair back behind her ear so that he had a clear view of her face. The touch of his hand sent a shiver racing through her. 'We need to talk about last night.'

She shook her head and forced herself to lift her blue eyes towards him. 'I think that last night should be left just as it was,' she murmured softly.

He opened his mouth to say something else and she gently placed her fingers over his lips. 'Last night was wonderful, Cole, but we both know that it can never happen again, that it was a wild but beautiful mistake—a bit like the rest of our relationship, really.' She gave a tremulous smile. Her pride wasn't going to allow her to break down; she was going to end things neatly with him, without losing her dignity. 'We both have other things in our life, other people who take priority. We are walking down different paths.'

The rugged planes of his attractive face looked stern. 'We don't have to walk down different paths, Lauren; there can be other nights like last night.'

Dark lashes hid the shimmering blue of her eyes from him. 'No, there can't, Cole.' Her voice was firm. She could never indulge in an affair with a married man. It was all or nothing as far as she was concerned, and, except for the fact that she was incredibly upset, she would have been angry at him for even suggesting it.

'You don't mean that, Lauren,' he said grimly. 'Look, we can have dinner together tonight and discuss this properly.' He gave her that lop-sided smile of his that made her heart want to melt. 'We can retire to your room afterwards and discuss it in even more detail.'

'I can hardly believe that you've just said that.' Now her eyes glimmered with anger.

'Can't you?' His eyes moved over the slender lines of her body in a suggestive way that made her face suffuse with colour. 'Look, I only need a couple more hours to have work finished. Then I suggest the two of us sneak out of here, go down to Phuket town——'

Lauren started to get to her feet. She wasn't about to start sneaking around; she didn't want a hole-and-corner kind of affair. Her eyes blazed up at him. 'I'm sorry, but I have other plans for this evening.'

He frowned. 'Who with?'

That was her cue to tell him she was leaving and this was goodbye. She pushed a trembling hand through her hair, but somehow the words wouldn't come.

'Lauren?' His voice held the rasping edge of impatience as he too got to his feet.

'Let's just leave it at that, Cole.' She started to swing away from him, but he grabbed her arm and somehow she ended up losing her balance and falling against the hard wall of his chest.

'That's better.' There was a smile in his voice now as his strong arms held her there. 'Now, I've had enough of this nonsense. We have a date for tonight. Seven o'clock.'

She allowed herself to relax against him, her eyes squeezed tightly shut. Seven tonight and she would be on her way to Bangkok.

'OK, Lauren?' He held her away from him and stared down at the pallor of her skin.

Before she could make any answer, the door opened and the man who had been working with Cole previously came back into the room. He was carrying a tray of coffee for them. 'Sorry to disturb you.' He placed the tray down on the table and started to retreat towards the door, looking a little bit embarrassed at having interrupted them.

'It's all right, you're not disturbing us.' Lauren took the opportunity to pull herself firmly away from Cole. 'I was just leaving.'

Cole's eyes narrowed on her. 'Have we a date for this evening?' He persisted with the conversation, completely ignoring the presence of the other man.

'Lauren?' He caught hold of her arm as she made to turn away. 'I asked you a question.'

Blue eyes clashed with dark. 'You know I'm not going to let you walk out of here until you say yes,' he told her, a hint of his arrogant smile playing around the firm lips.

Lauren stared up at him, her eyes filled with sadness. If only he loved her... if only things had been different.

'I'll call for you at your room. Seven sharp, all right?'

She nodded bleakly and he let her go. He watched her move towards the door and then, as she started to close it behind her, she heard him launch straight back into the conversation about the video that he had been having previously. 'We didn't cut that scene; Donna looked fabulous in it——'

The door shut off the rest of his words and for a moment Lauren leaned back against it, her eyes shut against the hot press of tears.

It took her a few moments to gather herself together and walk with her head held high towards the lifts. So much for being adult and telling Cole straight that she was leaving. Pride was such a fierce and rather stupid emotion, she thought dimly as she stepped into the lifts and pressed the button for the floor beneath. She hadn't been able to tell him to his face because she had known she would break down and she couldn't bear for him to see her like that; also there was a part of her that had been scared. If he had held her much longer, if he had kissed her, she might have weakened, she might have found herself agreeing to anything just to have a few stolen moments with him.

Her case was sitting neatly beside the desk in her bedroom. She sat down for a moment on the chair beside it and stared at it. It looked so final; she was leaving. For a moment she found herself remembering the way she had left Cole before. She had thought when she had walked away from him that day that her heart could never feel that pain again. Her lips twisted at the bitter irony of it. She was such a fool where Cole Adams was concerned...such a fool.

She pulled the hotel's writing paper towards her and scribbled him a note. Nothing personal, she said, but she found she had to return to London. Then she sat and stared at the words...so bleak, so cold after last night. It would help if she could stay angry with him, but her anger seemed to have drowned in her sadness.

Even the fury she had felt this morning when she had seen him holding Donna in his arms had receded. He loved the other woman; last night had been her fault entirely—she had thrown herself at him. She could hardly blame him for it.

The letter written, she sealed the envelope and picked up her bag.

She knocked on Jon's door on the way past to say goodbye but there was no reply so she made her way down to Reception. Amanda was there talking with one of the young receptionists. When she saw Lauren with her suitcase she looked startled.

'Lauren, are you leaving on your own?'

'Afraid so; I have to get back to London.' Lauren gave the other girl a brave smile.

Amanda frowned. 'Does Cole know you're leaving?'

Lauren shook her head. 'But I'm glad I've seen you before I go. Would you mind giving him this for me?' She passed over the letter for him.

'Sure thing, but why don't you wait and give it to him yourself?'

'No, I have a plane to catch.' Lauren glanced at her watch. 'In precisely two hours' time, so I'll have to get a move on.'

The receptionist interrupted them at that moment. 'Your taxi is here, Miss Martin.'

'Thank you.' Lauren smiled regretfully at Amanda. 'Thanks for everything, Amanda; it was lovely meeting you.'

Amanda nodded. 'If you're ever in Paris you must come and visit us.' The two girls embraced, then Lauren walked out into the late afternoon sunlight.

The taxi driver placed her bag in the boot and opened the door of the car for her. She was just climbing in when a voice halted her.

'Lauren, where are you going?' It was Donna, looking cool and very sophisticated in a mint-green linen suit.

'Back to London.' Lauren tried very hard to smile at the other girl.

One dark eyebrow lifted in surprise and green eyes narrowed in suspicion. 'What's brought on this sudden departure?'

Lauren shrugged. 'I have a lot of work waiting for me. Jon will take over here.'

'I see. Well, I suppose it's for the best, especially after last night. I know Cole still finds you attractive, Lauren, but it's nothing more than that. He loves me.' The girl's tone was brittle and direct.

There was an uncomfortable silence, Lauren desperately tried to gather herself together; she angled her chin a little higher and met the green eyes steadily. 'Well, I wish you both the very best.' There, that was extremely adult, she thought to herself. Extremely civilised, when all she really wanted to do was cry bitter tears.

'It's the twenty-fifth, in case you're wondering,' Donna suddenly blurted out as Lauren moved to get into the car.

Lauren stared at her. 'What is?'

'Our big day. Hopefully everything should still be on schedule, even though I have held things up a little with my... little accident with the video. I suppose you heard about that?'

Lauren nodded and her heart hammered chaotically against her ribcage. 'Yes, I heard. I wish you both the best, Donna.' Then she got into the taxi and, with a shadow of a smile at the other girl, told the driver she was ready to leave.

The car pulled slowly down the long driveway and Lauren sat dry-eyed looking out blindly at the colourful gardens. The twenty-fifth was only a few days away, then Cole and Donna would be married and starting out on their life together.

The security guards opened the large wrought-iron gates and the car sped out down the country roads in the direction of the airport.

She was on her way home and maybe one day she would be able to think of Cole without this terrible ache in her heart, although right at this moment she didn't think that was possible. In fact right at this moment Lauren was wondering how she would ever manage to carry on with her life, how she would ever be able to live without him.

CHAPTER TEN

BANGKOK was swathed in misty heat, the kind of heat that robbed you of energy and made even the simplest of tasks seem like hard work.

Lauren had been shopping. Not one of her better ideas, but as it was her last day in the country she had felt as if she should make some kind of effort to do something. Wandering around the air-conditioned, luxurious shops of River City would normally have been a sheer delight, but somehow Lauren couldn't summon up the enthusiasm. She had gazed at the beautiful hand-carved furniture, the exquisite *objets d'art*, and all she had thought about was Cole.

What would he have thought when he found her gone, when he'd read her letter? Would he have been relieved that she had gone, as Donna seemed to think, or would he have been disappointed not to be able to spend a few more illicit nights with her?

Had he wanted to continue their affair after he got married, or had she just been an interesting diversion for a couple of days?

The thoughts ran around and around in her head, plaguing her constantly. Tomorrow was January the twenty-fifth, the day that she would be flying home, the day that Cole would marry Donna, and she didn't think she could take it.

She wandered down the crowded streets, glancing at the market stalls with their fake designer watches and bags, and pushed a weary hand through her blonde hair.

'You like?' one of the stall-holders asked as he saw her looking at one of his bags. She smiled regretfully at the man and moved away. She was in no mood to start bartering for a handbag. In fact she was in no mood for anything. She stopped outside the entrance to an impressive-looking hotel and decided to try and get a taxi back to the Sheldon Hotel where she was staying while waiting for her flight.

Getting a taxi wasn't as easy as she had thought: they all seemed to be busy. A few tuk-tuks stopped for her, but the three-wheeled motorised little carriages were not suitable for the long distance back to the far side of the town. After a few moments of utter frustration she gave up on the idea and headed towards the river instead, deciding to take one of the river-buses back. It was a quicker way of travelling anyway as it cut out the heavy traffic chaos.

The sun was starting to sink in a huge orange ball of fire as Lauren stood on the floating platform that jutted into the river and waited for the boat. She was surrounded by people and still more were crowding down on to the platform. Apparently the boat they were waiting for was the last river-bus of the day, and it was starting to look a bit like rush-hour on the London Tubes. Lauren was just starting to wonder anxiously whether she should go back and try again to get a taxi. Then she heard the noisy chugging sound of the boat and the crowd surged forward, so that she was trapped firmly in their midst and it was too late to try and go back.

Lauren followed the crowd, leaping quickly from the platform to the boat before the man at the stern gave a long hard blast on a whistle and it took off with speed once more. Lauren wondered breathlessly if anyone had ever ended up in the river instead of the boat. They certainly didn't believe in allowing much time for getting on or off.

The boat was packed with all kinds of commuters: people making their way home from work, schoolchildren, saffron-robed monks, 'Farangs', as the Thai people called their foreign visitors, from all corners of the globe. Lauren had to fight her way through the crowds to be able to stand at the rail. She watched with a horrified kind of fascination as the boat pulled into a platform on the other side of the river now and allowed even more people on. Then, with a long whistle blast, they were off again.

Water slopped over the side of the rails as the boat was so heavily laden now that it was very low in the river. Lauren's hands clenched into tight fists as panic started to mount up inside her. If they allowed any more people on here the boat would surely sink without trace and there wouldn't be a hope in hell of anyone surviving. She stared down at the deep water and tried to think rationally. Of course they wouldn't sink; this boat made this same journey every day. Even so, as the boat started to pull in at another platform, Lauren started to move. She had had enough; all she could think about was getting off. That, however, was not so easy. She had not moved quickly enough and by the time she had fought her way to the stern the boat had accepted its passengers from the platform and moved out again. Now she was trapped in the thick of the crowd in the centre of the boat.

She squeezed her eyes tightly shut and willed herself to keep calm. Sometimes on the London Tubes at rush-hour she had felt similar bursts of panic, and she had always managed to come through it.

She opened her eyes and glanced around her. It was then that her glance locked with a pair of deep brown eyes. She felt a jolt of pure shock race down her spine and her heart seemed to increase its beat a hundred times. She was hallucinating, of course. Cole was miles away preparing for his wedding. She closed her eyes and opened them again, but he was still there. The rugged features, so dear and so familiar, were set in a mask of determination as he made his way through the crowds to stand next to her.

'Cole,' she whispered his name, and then he was pulling her in close against a broad hard chest. Maybe this was a dream, maybe she would wake up in a moment and find him gone. But the arms that were holding her were strong and protective and very real. She swallowed hard and then, to her complete mortification, broke down in tears.

Cole held her tightly against his chest. 'You're all right, sweetheart. You're safe now.'

She barely heard the words he whispered against her ear over the din of the noisy engine and the loud thumping of her heart. She wasn't sure how long she stood there clinging to him—all she was aware of was the warm, protective feeling of being in the circle of his arms. Then he moved her firmly and guided her through the crowds up to the stern of the boat. It pulled in at another stop and, holding on to her firmly, Cole helped her off.

Even though they were now safely back on firm ground Lauren couldn't help shaking. She was literally trembling from head to toe, and the tears refused to stop flowing. She didn't know if she was so upset because of the fear she had felt among the crush of the boat or whether it was seeing Cole again like this when she had thought she never would again. Cole cradled her gently in strong arms and made low soothing sounds against her ear.

Feeling extremely foolish and vulnerable, Lauren fought to get herself back under control and pulled away from him after an agonising couple of minutes. 'I'm...I'm sorry,' she murmured lamely, wiping a trembling hand over her wet face and staring down at the ground. 'I'm really sorry.'

'What for?' Cole asked gently. 'Running out on me in Phuket? I don't know if I'm going to forgive you for that, Lauren. I'm not used to being stood up.' There was a gentle hint of indulgent humour in his tone as he took a crisp white handkerchief from his pocket and handed it to her.

She accepted it gratefully and noisily blew her nose. Her mind refused to function properly; all she could do was repeat herself again and tell him she was sorry.

With an exasperated sigh he pulled her back in against the hard length of his body. 'What am I going to do with you, Lauren Martin?' he murmured against her ear. 'What am I going to do with you?'

He held her slightly away from him and stared down at the tear-stained face. 'Are you going to tell me why you sneaked away from me in Phuket?'

When she made no answer he shook his head. 'I rang your editor when I discovered you'd gone. I don't think he's too pleased with you.'

Lauren's lips twisted ruefully. She was damn sure Warren would not be pleased with her. 'I think I've probably lost my job,' she said with a loud sniff.

He tipped her chin upwards and stared into her bright, tear-drenched eyes. 'Are you bothered?'

She shrugged and once more the tears started to flow. 'I don't know what to think,' she murmured brokenly.

'Come on, let's get you back to the hotel and I'll tell you what to think,' Cole said with a teasing smile.

'I don't need anyone to help me think,' she snapped automatically, and he grinned.

'That's better. Shall we go inside?' He nodded towards the hotel they were standing outside and for the first time Lauren looked around her.

They were standing outside the Sheldon Hotel. Lauren frowned. 'Did you know I was staying here?'

'Jon told me I might find you here,' he told her drily. 'I think I might have changed my mind about that guy after all; he's OK.'

'I see.' Lauren desperately tried to assimilate this piece of information. Then shook her head. 'Cole, what are you doing here?'

'Looking for you.' He caught hold of her arm. 'Come on—as you don't seem to want to go inside, we'll go around and sit on the terrace.'

She allowed him to lead her around to the side of the hotel where some steps led towards the long terrace. It was deserted and looked extremely pretty in the dusky pink glow of evening. Candle-light flickered on the tables, reflecting on highly polished silverware laid ready for evening diners. Coloured lights twinkled along the balustrades that separated the terrace from the dark gleaming water of the Chao Phya.

Cole selected a table at the very edge of the terrace and pulled a chair out for her. She took it silently, her mind in complete chaos. She still couldn't quite believe he was here; she felt as if this was some dream, and at any moment she would wake up. And she couldn't understand for the life of her why he should come looking for her.

A waiter came over to see if they wanted anything, and Cole ordered a bottle of champagne.

'A bit early for celebrations, isn't it?' Lauren asked in a bleak tone as she watched the waiter disappear.

He frowned. 'Maybe.' His voice held a note of caution.

'Tomorrow is the day for opening champagne, isn't it?' she persisted and for a moment she allowed herself to meet his eyes across the table.

One eyebrow lifted. 'Tomorrow...?' Then his face cleared as he realised to what she was referring. He shook his head. 'Who told you about that?'

'Donna.' She looked out over the river. The pink glow of twilight was fading rapidly into the darkness of night. 'I suppose she's here with you?'

'Then you suppose wrong,' he said bluntly.

'Where is she?' One slender hand clenched unconsciously as it rested on the table. Why was she asking such a foolish question? Did it matter where the woman was? The fact remained that tomorrow Donna would be Mrs Cole Adams. They had probably decided not to spend their last night of freedom under the same roof. That was considered unlucky.

Their champagne arrived. Cole indicated to the waiter to leave it for him to uncork, and once more they were left alone.

'Does it matter where she is?' Cole returned easily to her question.

Lauren shrugged slim shoulders, her eyes still locked out over the river. The tropical heat of the night was intense; there wasn't a ruffle in the silky smooth water, it was like jet-black Thai silk. Like the dress she had worn the night Cole had made love to her.

'Lauren?' Cole reached out and caught hold of her slender wrist. 'Why did you sneak out on me in Phuket?'

'I didn't sneak out on you.' Stubbornly she refused to turn her gaze away from the view and back towards him. 'I just decided that it was best I didn't hang around. You know what they say about two's company,' she quipped lightly.

He frowned. 'No, Lauren, I don't follow you at all. I thought after the night we spent together that you felt something for me. I thought maybe it meant that you were still in love with me.'

Her face blazed with colour as she swung furious blue eyes back towards him. 'Does Donna know you're here asking me questions like that?'

'No,' he answered her calmly. 'It's none of Donna's business.' He reached across and took hold of her hand. 'Lauren, sweetheart, I nearly went out of my mind when I found you were gone.'

'Stop it, Cole.' Her eyes filled with tears again and she tried to pull her hand away from his, but he wouldn't allow her. 'Let me go.' She whispered the words in a husky, broken voice.

'No, I don't want to let you go.' He said the words in a low undertone. 'I know you care about me; you couldn't have kissed me the way you did if you felt nothing for me.' Dark eyes raked over her delicate features, noting every flicker of her expression. 'Jon told me that you left because you still loved me.'

Pride and pain shimmered in her eyes, and she looked away from him. 'He had no right to say anything like that.'

'Well, I did bribe him. Promised him exclusive pictures of my intended bride, so don't be too angry with him.' There was just a note of humour in the deep, steady voice.

Anger was too mild a word for how she felt for Jon at that moment. How could he humiliate her like that?

'Well?' Cole continued huskily. 'Is it true: do you love me?'

She shook her head, feeling embarrassed and uncomfortable. Two high spots of colour burnt in her cheeks as she looked away from him. 'You are so damn arrogant, Cole. Sometimes I... I just hate you,' she told him in a voice that vibrated with raw emotion.

'No, you don't. You couldn't have made love to me that night at the hotel if you hated me.' He reached and caught hold of her chin in a firm yet gentle grip. She knew that he could feel the trembling that racked her body through the smooth softness of her skin. Desperately she strove for control and some way to save her pride, but no words would come to her rescue.

'Maybe you thought you hated me once... with good reason, I'm loath to admit. But when we made love all hatred ceased to exist——'

'Cole, stop it!' she cut across him with real anguish. 'I don't know what game you're playing, but——'

'I'm not playing games, Laurie. I've never been more serious in my life. When we made love——'

She lifted her hand to push his away. 'We didn't make love; we had sex. There is a difference.' Her voice was bitter with emotion.

'Of course there is.' His voice remained calm and steady. 'And I made love to you, Lauren.' He stressed the words gently, then lifted her hand and rested it against the smooth silk of his shirt so that she could feel the steady beat of his heart through the trembling softness of her hands. 'I made love to you with all my heart, all my soul. You know the Buddhists have a saying? It goes, "Hatreds never cease by hatreds in this world. By love alone they cease."' His eyes sought and held hers. 'I love you, Lauren; I always have and I always will. I was all set to tell you that when you first came out here...' He shrugged self-consciously. 'Then Jon seemed to be on the scene, and pride and jealousy just wouldn't allow me get the right words out.'

She didn't say anything; her breath seemed to have frozen in her throat. Her blue eyes gleamed over-bright, her dark lashes were wet with tears.

Cole squeezed her hand. 'I had all these plans to get you out here and win you back, and they just all went to pieces when I saw you with Jon.' He raked a hand through his strong dark hair. 'Please tell me you love me, Lauren; it's tearing me apart thinking that I might lose you again.'

'I just don't understand,' she whispered, and one stray tear trickled down her cheek. 'I thought you were going to marry Donna.'

He smiled. 'The only person that I had plans to marry was you, Lauren. Totally arrogant of me—I realised that as soon as you arrived out here.' He grinned boyishly. 'You never were predictable. I should have taken that stubborn, independent streak of yours into consideration when I concocted that story about a wedding.'

'But Donna told me.' Lauren brushed a trembling hand over her face to wipe the tears away. 'She told me that you had an affair with her before you got involved with me and then again after we split up. She told me that you had plans to get married; she even told me the date you were getting married...she said the twenty-fifth——'

'Well, she was lying,' Cole cut across her furiously, his voice harshly angry now. 'The only plans I had for Donna were strictly on a business level. There has never been anything between us. In fact yesterday morning after I discovered what she had done with the video I told her I didn't want anything more to do with her career. I found her manner and her conduct totally unprofessional.'

'But I saw you out in the gardens with her that morning,' Lauren murmured in confusion. 'She had her arms around you——'

'She was begging me for another chance with her career,' he put in abruptly. 'I told her I'd think about it...Lauren?' he trailed off uncertainly as she bent her head away from him. 'You do believe me, don't you? I swear to you that it's the truth. Donna has never meant anything to me.'

She nodded but couldn't trust herself to speak; there was a wealth of happiness exploding in deep emotion inside her and tears of joy and relief were pouring down her face. How could she doubt the sincerity in that deep voice? It shone through his every word.

'Lauren?' He reached out a hand and tipped her face up towards his. He swore softly at the tears that he saw. 'Oh, Lauren, I don't want to hurt you; I reckon I've done enough of that in the past. Please don't cry.' He reached his hand up gently to smooth away her tears.

'I'm not crying,' she told him breathlessly.

'No? You could have fooled me.'

Some other diners came out on to the terrace and Cole caught her hand firmly. 'Come on, let's go somewhere we can be alone. What I have to say to you isn't for the public's ears.' He picked up the bottle of champagne and led her back into the hotel.

One of the porters on the door smiled warmly at him. 'I see you found your lady.'

'I certainly did, and I'm not about to let her go again,' Cole replied with a firmness to his voice that melted Lauren completely.

When they stepped into the lift Cole turned and looked at her.

She put a self-conscious hand to her face. She had cried so much that she must look awful, she thought despondently. 'How did the porter know you were looking for me?' It was something to say just to cover her embarrassment.

He smiled. 'He was the one who told me you had taken a taxi to River City. I've been searching for you all afternoon—not an easy task in Bangkok.' He grinned at her. 'The river-bus was a last-minute decision when I couldn't get a cab back—I couldn't believe my luck when I spotted you among the crowds.'

'I'm glad you were there,' she murmured breathlessly. 'I'm glad that you're here.'

He put out a hand and stopped the lift between floors. 'Say that again,' he ordered huskily.

'I'm glad you're here...' Anything else she had to say was crushed beneath the tenderness of his kiss.

When he pulled away, he brushed away the wetness of her tears and then held her close. 'Tell me you forgive me, Lauren,' he murmured next to her ear. 'I need to hear you say it. I don't think I've stopped blaming myself about the baby, about the way I treated you.'

Lauren closed her eyes and breathed in the heady scent of being close to him. 'You know I forgive you, Cole.' She smiled sadly. 'It was myself that I found hard to forgive. I made such a mess...'

'No, Lauren, *I* made the mess. Me and my stubborn ideas. When you asked me how I felt about a serious commitment to you I guess I just panicked. We had been so happy just living together that I was frightened to change anything; I suppose I was frightened of losing you. But my cold-blooded behaviour managed to do that anyway.'

His dark eyes were shadowed with bleak remembrance as he stared down at her. 'When you mentioned wanting commitment and a family, I never for one moment suspected that you might be pregnant. I just thought you were rushing things. I suppose I have a thing about that. I had always told myself that I wouldn't bring a child into this world unless everything was right. I would have to have time for my child; I would give it all the things that my own childhood lacked——'

'I didn't know you had a bad childhood.' Lauren pulled away from him and stared up at him with startled wide eyes.

His mouth twisted grimly. 'Oh, yes. My parents were career people. I think they both resented my unplanned and unwelcome appearance late on in their marriage. I swore I'd be different to any child of mine.' He looked down at her with grim eyes. 'I was so heavily involved in my career, Lauren, and I used to worry that you were missing yours. I wanted to just take things cautiously and slowly. I guess I just plain panicked.'

Lauren shook her head. 'The only thing I missed was you,' she told him softly. 'We seemed to have grown so apart during that time.'

He nodded. 'And it was all my fault. I realised that once you were gone. My work had taken me over so much that I just wasn't even thinking clearly. The world tour took a hell of a lot out of me, then there was a new album——' He broke off and shook his head ruefully. 'All those things seemed so important at that time, and then you left me and I suddenly realised just how unimportant they were compared with you.'

'Oh, Cole.' Lauren buried her head in against his broad chest. 'I love you so much.'

'You don't know how long I've waited to hear you say that.' Cole held on to her with fiercely protective arms. 'I've been so consumed with jealousy watching you and Jon together; you seem to have so much in common and you got on so well... it scared the hell out of me.'

She smiled sadly. 'Funny, I thought exactly the same about you and Donna.' She met his eyes steadily. 'There has never been anything between Jon and me; we're colleagues, nothing more.'

'I know; Jon put me straight on a few things back in Phuket.' He pulled her in so tightly against him that for a moment she thought she wouldn't be able to breathe. 'Do you think you could give me another chance, Lauren?'

She smiled tremulously against his chest. 'You know that right now I'd give you anything you want,' she told him huskily.

'Now that sounds very promising.' His head moved down and his lips trailed over her cheek, then found hers in a long, hungry kiss. One hand reached for the button of the lift. 'I suppose we'd better retire somewhere a little more comfortable,' he whispered against her ear. 'Then you can make me some more promises.'

'Well, I warn you, I only make ones I can keep,' she whispered back.

'I should think so too.'

Later... much later, when they lay entwined in silk sheets, their bodies close, Lauren pulled away from him slightly to look down into the languorous depths of his deep eyes. 'By the way,' she murmured sleepily, 'what's happening tomorrow?'

'Tomorrow?' He frowned slightly, for a moment his brain still engaged in the deeply pleasurable world of their lovemaking.

'Yes, tomorrow. Donna said that something was arranged for tomorrow. I presumed it was your wedding arrangement.'

Cole looked completely horrified. 'Certainly not! Tomorrow my last album will be released. That must be what she was referring to.'

'Oh.' Lauren snuggled back down against him, feeling happy again. 'So it is true—you *are* definitely giving up your singing.'

'Oh, yes. No more tours for me. I have other more important things I want to be doing.'

'Are you quite sure you want to give up all that? It was so important to you.'

'Laurie, I have never been more sure of anything in my life.' He whispered the words firmly and without hesitation against the softness of her hair. 'From now on I'm a family man first and foremost.'

'Family?' Blue eyes locked with dark and he nodded firmly.

'Well, you are going to marry me, aren't you?' he demanded huskily. 'After all, we do owe Warren a story, and I did promise Jon the exclusive.'

'Oh, Cole.' She wound her hands up and through the jet-black darkness of his thick hair.

'I hope that's a yes...' For a moment his voice was uncertain.

'It is a most definite yes,' she answered with complete and utter certainty.

Next Month's Romances

Each month you can choose from a wide variety of romance with Mills & Boon. Below are the new titles to look out for next month, why not ask either Mills & Boon Reader Service or your Newsagent to reserve you a copy of the titles you want to buy — just tick the titles you would like and either post to Reader Service or take it to any Newsagent and ask them to order your books.

Please save me the following titles:	Please tick	√
BREAKING POINT	Emma Darcy	
SUCH DARK MAGIC	Robyn Donald	
AFTER THE BALL	Catherine George	
TWO-TIMING MAN	Roberta Leigh	
HOST OF RICHES	Elizabeth Power	
MASK OF DECEPTION	Sara Wood	
A SOLITARY HEART	Amanda Carpenter	
AFTER THE FIRE	Kay Gregory	
BITTERSWEET YESTERDAYS	Kate Proctor	
YESTERDAY'S PASSION	Catherine O'Connor	
NIGHT OF THE SCORPION	Rosemary Carter	
NO ESCAPING LOVE	Sharon Kendrick	
OUTBACK LEGACY	Elizabeth Duke	
RANSACKED HEART	Jayne Bauling	
STORMY REUNION	Sandra K. Rhoades	
A POINT OF PRIDE	Liz Fielding	

If you would like to order these books in addition to your regular subscription from Mills & Boon Reader Service please send £1.70 per title to: Mills & Boon Reader Service, P.O. Box 236, Croydon, Surrey, CR9 3RU, quote your Subscriber No:..
(If applicable) and complete the name and address details below. Alternatively, these books are available from many local Newsagents including W.H.Smith, J.Menzies, Martins and other paperback stockists from 12th March 1993.

Name:..
Address:...
....Post Code:............................

To Retailer: If you would like to stock M&B books please contact your regular book/magazine wholesaler for details.

You may be mailed with offers from other reputable companies as a result of this application.
If you would rather not take advantage of these opportunities please tick box ☐

THE PERFECT GIFT FOR MOTHER'S DAY

Specially selected for you – four tender and heartwarming Romances written by popular authors.

LEGEND OF LOVE -
Melinda Cross

AN IMPERFECT AFFAIR -
Natalie Fox

LOVE IS THE KEY -
Mary Lyons

LOVE LIKE GOLD -
Valerie Parv

Mills & Boon

Available from February 1993   Price: £6.80

Available from Boots, Martins, John Menzies, W.H. Smith, most supermarkets and other paperback stockists. Also available from Mills & Boon Reader Service, PO Box 236, Thornton Road, Croydon, Surrey CR9 3RU. (UK Postage & Packing free)

Mills & Boon

4 FREE

Romances and 2 FREE gifts just for you!

*You can enjoy all the
heartwarming emotion of true love for FREE!
Discover the heartbreak and the happiness, the emotion and
the tenderness of the modern relationships in
Mills & Boon Romances.*

*We'll send you 4 captivating Romances as a special offer from
Mills & Boon Reader Service, along with the chance to have
6 Romances delivered to your door each month.*

Claim your FREE books and gifts overleaf...

An irresistible offer from Mills & Boon

Here's a personal invitation from Mills & Boon Reader Service, to become a regular reader of Romances. To welcome you, we'd like you to have 4 books, a CUDDLY TEDDY and a special MYSTERY GIFT absolutely FREE.

Then you could look forward each month to receiving 6 brand new Romances, delivered to your door, postage and packing free! Plus our free Newsletter featuring author news, competitions, special offers and much more.

This invitation comes with no strings attached. You may cancel or suspend your subscription at any time, and still keep your free books and gifts.

It's so easy. Send no money now. Simply fill in the coupon below and post it to -
**Reader Service, FREEPOST,
PO Box 236, Croydon, Surrey CR9 9EL.**

NO STAMP REQUIRED

Free Books Coupon

Yes! Please rush me 4 free Romances and 2 free gifts! Please also reserve me a Reader Service subscription. If I decide to subscribe I can look forward to receiving 6 brand new Romances each month for just £10.20, postage and packing free. If I choose not to subscribe I shall write to you within 10 days - I can keep the books and gifts whatever I decide. I may cancel or suspend my subscription at any time. I am over 18 years of age.

Ms/Mrs/Miss/Mr_____ EP31R

Address _____

_____

Postcode_____ Signature _____

Offer expires 31st May 1993. The right is reserved to refuse an application and change the terms of this offer. Readers overseas and in Eire please send for details. Southern Africa write to Book Services International Ltd, P.O. Box 42654, Craighall, Transvaal 2024. You may be mailed with offers from other reputable companies as a result of this application.

If you would prefer not to share in this opportunity, please tick box ☐